If it had been meant to be a hug, it failed completely. Their mouths met hungrily and Marian pulled Liddy's hips against her own. Their kiss was immediate union, lips, tongues, moans, air, mingling instantly, as if they had never stopped making love to each other.

Liddy's cheeks were quickly wet with rain from Marian's hair. Marian felt the drops against her hands as she cupped Liddy's face and kissed her again, and again, tasting her mouth. She rubbed her lips against Liddy's and heard, for the first time in years, her name whispered in wonder.

She licked the line of Liddy's jaw, then nipped her earlobe. And felt Liddy's body stiffen in her arms, then arch in a curve of offering.

WRITING AS KARIN KALLMAKER:

One Degree of Separation
Maybe Next Time
Substitute for Love
Frosting on the Cake
Unforgettable
Watermark
Making Up for Lost Time
Embrace in Motion
Wild Things
Painted Moon
Car Pool
Paperback Romance
Touchwood
In Every Port
All the Wrong Places (forthcoming from Bella After Dark)
Sugar (forthcoming from Bella Books)

WRITING AS LAURA ADAMS:

Christabel

The Tunnel of Light Trilogy:
Sleight of Hand
Seeds of Fire

Daughters of Pallas:
Night Vision
The Dawning

One Degree
of Separation

by
Karin Kallmaker

Bella
BOOKS

2003

Bella Books, Inc.
P.O. Box 10543
Tallahassee, FL 32302

Printed in the United States of America
First Edition

Editor: Christi Cassidy
Cover designer: Bonnie Liss (Phoenix Graphics)

ISBN 1-931513-30-9

For Maria,
who found my future in the card catalogs at Berkeley Main

Fourteen and Fortunately no longer a Felony

This book would not be possible—indeed, information would not be ours for the asking—if not for the passion of librarians in preserving our freedom to read.

My eternal gratitude goes to MJ Lowe for her generous, humorous and tireless attempts to teach me the intricate necessities of library sciences and the tantalizing mysteries of information arts.

ABOUT THE AUTHOR

Karin Kallmaker admits that her first crush on a woman was the local librarian. Just remembering the pencil through the loose, attractive bun makes her warm. She was perhaps more permanently marked by watching that same librarian, some years later, argue respectfully but passionately with a man who had thrown away a book he'd checked out, claiming it was obscene.

Maybe it was the librarian's influence, but for whatever reason, at the age of 16 Karin fell into the arms of her first and only sweetheart. There's a certain symmetry to the fact that ten years later, after seeing the film *Desert Hearts*, her sweetheart descended on the Berkeley Public Library to find some of "those" books. In the old-style card catalogs, author card "Rule, Jane" led to subject card "Lesbianism—Fiction" and then on to book after self-affirming book by and about lesbians. These books were the encouragement Karin needed to forget the so-called "mainstream" and spin her first romance for lesbians. That manuscript became her first novel, *In Every Port*.

The happily-ever-after couple now lives in the San Francisco Bay Area, and became Mom and Moogie to Kelson in 1995 and Eleanor in 1997. They celebrated their twenty-seventh anniversary in 2004.

All of Karin's work can now be found at Bella Books. Details and background about her novels, and her other pen name, Laura Adams, can be found at her own web site.

1

Monday evening, June 2:

I will not damage the rude patrons or the annoying heterosexual coworker.

Trombone continues to throw up in my shoes. Professor Hill has chewed up the crotch of yet another pair of panties. It's been so long since anyone was down there I've probably turned to liverwurst.

I'm never going to move up if I don't get my M.L.S., so I'm going to get my M.L.S. It's not like it'll cut much into my social life.

HER is still the only woman I want. As usual, I feel stupid and pathetic for wanting HER.

Someone will die if my period doesn't start tomorrow.

❧

"We have to have lunch. Today." Marian knew that cement tone in Ellie's voice.

"But I don't know more than what I said," Marian protested. She took her mug of hot tea out of the microwave and set it down on the table in the break room.

"You may not realize what you know."

"You sound like an interrogator. I don't have time for lunch today. Bill's out sick." Marian wanted to kick herself. She ought to have known that Ellie would go into hyper-hunt mode the moment she found out.

"I thought Bill the Boor's being out would make you happy. So celebrate by having lunch with me."

Marian steadied herself with a deep breath. "When Jersey stopped in this morning, she said that Amy said the woman was getting a stack pass at the Psych Library. So she'll be here for a while."

"Yeah, but I want first shot at her. C'mon, Marian. Fresh meat in the summer? That never happens! You and I have a chance for once. You know that Jersey left the library and told at least five student dykes. Amy told five faculty dykes after she told Jersey, you *know* she did. And all of them told five dykes. By tonight every dyke in Iowa City is going to know."

Though she spoke through gritted teeth, Marian thought she managed to sound almost normal. "Dinner. I can meet you for dinner."

Clearly surprised, Ellie replied, "Well, okay. That'll do, I guess. Where?"

"You decide. I can't make decisions today."

"Oh." Ellie clicked her tongue against her teeth, a sound Marian found as annoying on the phone as she did in person. "I see. Amani's?"

Amani's chocolate cake was exactly what Marian needed. "At seven," she confirmed. Eric wandered into the staff room and looked hopefully at the phone. "Break's over. Gotta go."

Back at the reference desk, Marian surreptitiously unwrapped a Dove dark chocolate bite. On a day like today it was medicinal. Besides, it was heart healthy and she had a link to the research study to prove it.

She had just finished savoring the last bitter aftertaste when a patron paused at the desk. She pushed the chocolate's wrapper into the back pocket of her tailored khaki shorts and smiled pleasantly. "May I help you locate a resource?"

The youth's slouch and greasy hair was at odds with a shy smile. "Could you help me, I guess, I want to please know how would I address a letter to the Queen. Of England. Please."

Books and covers, Marian thought. "We have several texts on etiquette, but a simple Web search might be fastest. Did you want just that question answered or are you interested in the topic of social etiquette with monarchs?"

"It's for a school sociology project. My final."

Given the date, Marian thought he'd left his research a little late. High schools were nearly out. "Then for thorough research I think you'll want the text."

Marian led the boy to an open terminal. "Have you used the public library system before?" The boy cleared his throat, but Marian didn't know quite what to make of the noise that came out. Now she recognized him. He worked afternoons at the Java House.

"No? Here's the catalog browser and you can use the Internet browser as well. It's of course free and there's no enforced time limit. Starting tomorrow, new software will limit you to two hours of Internet access per day. Try a catalog search for etiquette and I think we'll see some useful guides. Sorry about the mouse. Just click three times." Tech Services was taking its time getting a new one.

Even though the day was not going well, the orderly precision of the Dewey Decimal System was comforting as always to Marian. She patiently explained how the cataloging system worked and led him to the nonfiction shelves.

"So all these books in this area could be helpful because they're numbered the same?" The boy looked a bit like he'd found the Mother Lode. Marian was gratified to have been the one to have shown him the Dewey magic, but she was simultaneously peeved that he hadn't been taught in school. As pleasant as teaching the system could be, it was not the be-all and end-all of her career choice.

"Precisely, and related subjects, like cultural standards, are adjacent. The very last Dewey entry, by the way, is the nine hundred ninety-nine series—extraterrestrial."

"Cool."

She was very pleased he hadn't grabbed the book she'd pointed out initially and bolted. "If you find your question hasn't been completely answered, feel free to return to the reference desk. Good luck with your paper," she concluded cheerily.

Safely back at the desk, Marian congratulated herself for not killing anyone so far.

"I can't find the phone book I need."

It was an effort, but Marian plastered a smile on her face. Over the patron's shoulder she saw Eric, travel mug in hand, veer abruptly toward the magazines, leaving her to deal with the woman she privately thought of as the Lead Bitch from the Seventh Dimension of Bitch Universe. "How pleasant to see you again. What area were you looking for?"

Seventh Dimension Bitch tossed her fluffy blonde hair over her shoulder. There was something in the way she did it that made Marian absolutely certain that she should feel inadequate about her own short, dark, unremarkable hair. The woman had all the attitude of Trombone, but likely none of the purring. "Dallas, of course."

"Of course," Marian echoed. "I'm sorry, but the Iowa City Public Library no longer carries phone books for areas outside of the state. But you can use several different sources on the Internet. I'd be happy—"

"Never mind! You people never have what I want." The departing flounce ruffled several papers onto the floor.

After tidying, Marian reached surreptitiously for another square of chocolate. Eric, the chickenshit, was back. Under her breath she said, "How long do you think it would take for someone to die from being repeatedly stapled?"

4

"It's not worth it. I don't want to visit you in jail."

"But I look good in orange."

"You look like a cadaver in orange."

Marian became aware of the tinny treble from a pair of headphones, but no one in sight had a pair on. She'd have to hunt for the culprit.

A cell phone shrilled from the direction of adult nonfiction, sending razors up her spine. "I'm at the library, so I can't talk long," a man's voice boomed.

"I'll go," Eric said.

"No, I got it. Days like today these cards save lives."

She slipped the cell-phone user the first card, which politely asked the patron to end the call or to step outside, and nodded pleasantly at the man's annoyed face. Had he no clue at all that everyone in the vicinity could hear his opinion of last night's date? She waited until he shuffled slowly toward the exit, then let her ears guide her toward the still audible static and bass of headphones.

The young woman read the card in surprise but mouthed an apology and turned the volume down sufficiently so that Marian could no longer hear anything.

Fair enough, Marian thought. She gave the patron a thumbs-up and went back to the desk. She had another hour of desk time before she could retire to the shared workspace in the back to review new acquisitions. No one had had to be gutted and grilled. It was a relief.

Eric wasn't there, but Seventh Dimension Bitch was.

It took a very deep breath to find even a businesslike smile. She dealt with the next series of statements about the library system's inadequacies without losing her cool, though she felt like a cartoon character with steam coming out of her ears.

Please, she thought, let my period start now. Or someone is going to die.

Eric had moved all the staplers to his end of the desk.

⤷⤶

"I want to know absolutely everything Jersey said." Ellie wasted no time taking a long sip from the Manhattan she'd ordered.

Marian squinted at the menu, looking for something light as preparation to diving face first into the Chocolate Thunder cake. "Why can't you call Jersey yourself? It's not like you don't have her number."

"Jersey isn't reliable on the details, you know that."

"I think she is. It's Sandy who said Jersey couldn't remember the right name during, but I don't see how that affects her recall when she's out of bed."

"When it comes to fresh meat in the dating market, I need accuracy, that's all. I tried Amy, but she wasn't home. Besides . . ." Ellie sighed. "Jersey has been looking too good to me lately, and she's with Terry. I shouldn't flirt with her as much as I do."

Marian looked over the menu in alarm. "You wouldn't, would you?"

"What? Sleep with Jersey?"

"Yeah. That would be just . . . *weird*."

"Frankly, my dear, it can be kind of kinky to think about. It's not like Sandy spilled the whole Jersey story, but I do know a bit about what she's like."

"You could really be with an ex's ex?"

Ellie stirred her Manhattan. "In this town how can you avoid it? Well, *you* avoid it by not dating at all."

"Next thing you know you'll tell me you've slept with both women in a couple."

Ellie got her you-have-no-idea-the-things-I've-done smirk. "I have the sense at least not to tell."

"You haven't."

"Not saying. But believe me, about now I'm desperate enough to do it again."

"Ellie!"

"Forget I said that." Ellie did not look in the least bit remorseful.

"You'll get a reputation."

6

"Your inner prude is showing. I already have a reputation." Marian wasn't fooled by Ellie's nonchalant air. "You and I are the only single women over thirty-five in this town. That is, besides Sandy, and she's my ex now even if we're still living together. So why should I forego the willing but perhaps entangled ones?"

It's not right, Marian wanted to say. Yes, Inner Prude was clear about that. Inner Historian, keeper of the Iowa City dance card, wanted to know who. Inner Slut wanted to know if it had been good. "Maybe I'm not meant to live in the modern era."

"Maybe you need to put sex into perspective. It doesn't have to be the ultimate exercise of love. Love doesn't even have to enter into the picture."

"But shouldn't it?"

"Only in a Hallmark card. What has a desire for monogamy done for either of us? I date too much and you don't date at all." Ellie yanked at the front of her blouse. "I think I've gained weight. Great. Just great."

Marian knew her cue. She said heartily, "You look tasty, as always. Femme on a Triscuit, positively edible." They'd been best friends for more than half their lives, and such reassurance was second nature to Marian. Ellie had the looks and figure that were universally described as attractive by men and women alike. She had a flashy style and brash confidence about her looks that had always eluded Marian. Regardless, she needed to be reminded of her assets, just as Marian occasionally needed to be told she had a brain.

Maybe, Marian thought, I could just have chocolate cake for dinner. And another slice for dessert.

"Sorry. Sharing the house with Sandy is starting to get to me. Celibacy is starting to get to me. I've even been thinking about Sandy again, and that would *so* give her the wrong idea."

"Well, I'm not sleeping with you." Damn, with her period so close it was actually tempting. Useless hormones.

"All the more reason for you and me to find out who this new woman is and get busy. You know Carrie will sniff her out in less than three days with that voodoo thing she does."

"It's not voodoo, it's Wicca, and you can't use Wicca that way."

"How would you know?"

"I'm a librarian. Besides, Carrie doesn't go after just anybody. It's just that when she does she usually succeeds. "Marian closed the menu. "Chicken medallions sound good. Light."

"One of these days I am not going to let you win an argument with that chintzy librarian credential."

Marian allowed herself a small smile. "Hey, you can disdain my master's in history all you like, but I must inform you that you're talking to a future Master of Library and Information Science."

"Since when?"

"Since when I sign the check and fill out the paperwork. And get a reference from Mary Jane."

"Girlfriend!" Ellie lifted her drink and clinked it to Marian's water glass. "Congrats."

Grinning, Marian thought it wise to admonish Ellie further. "So you'll have to be careful when you call my bluff. If I'm right, you'll never hear the end—"

"Shut up." Ellie frowned at the menu. "I love this place but I can't afford it. Neither of my careers is paying well enough right now. I'm behind in billing insurance companies for the physical therapy work. So I took on Jenny's guest bathroom plumbing for the cash. End result is I have no time to bill insurance. Would you be willing to split dinner?"

"Can we get a salad, too?"

"Spinach?"

"I will not share my cake."

"I'm not sharing my drink, so we're even." Ellie studied her manicure for a moment, frowning. "Frankly, sleeping with both women in a couple is damned appealing right now. Preferably at the same time, on a great big bed with every imaginable assistive device, thank you."

"Don't dangle images like that in front of me today." Inner Slut pouted at Marian's refusal to consider the fantasy. Not here, she soothed. You know we can't have that particular fantasy here.

The restaurant door opened, letting in a brief whiff of early evening humidity. Marian blinked. "Amy and Hemma just walked in."

Ellie turned around to wave. "Speaking of couples I'd sleep with, as if that would ever happen. Monogamy is such a bore. At least Amy can tell me about the new babe. You're no help."

Inadequate yet again, Marian thought. While Ellie was twisted around to wave at Amy, Marian snagged Ellie's cocktail and managed several swallows before she returned it to its place atop the petite napkin.

Hemma was wearing an aqua linen blouse Marian hadn't seen before. "That's a great color on you," Marian told her after their hello.

"You are so good for my ego, thank you. Tell me they have choco-late cake tonight." Hemma's deep black eyes sparkled in the low light.

Horrified, Marian said, "I haven't asked. You don't suppose—"

"They have cake, I can see a slice on the tray." Amy slipped a bracing arm around Hemma's waist. "Cake is essential tonight."

Ellie grinned. "Tell me about it. Marian's got PMS so bad she can't even scam with me about that new woman."

Marian felt a blush start under her hairline. She prayed it didn't show in the low light. "I'm not in the mood to scam."

Hemma smiled in her understanding way. "You're coming to dinner Thursday as usual?"

"I'm there unless you've finally decided to change the locks after all these years."

Hemma patted Marian's shoulder. "You could get in anyway. You know which windows don't latch."

After searching her friends' faces for any sign that she wasn't wel-come, Marian made her hypersensitive PMS self relax. Their almost weekly ritual of Thursday night dinner was of such long standing that it had survived Robyn Vaughn's arrival in Marian's life and Robyn Vaughn's departure. But there was always a chance that they had tired of her company, or that they'd figured out how much the ritual meant to Marian.

Amy was finishing her detailed description of the woman she'd seen getting a stack pass. "Not quite your height. Closer to Marian's than yours."

"That short?" Ellie glanced at Marian as if she'd never considered Marian's height before.

"I am not short," Marian protested. "I am exactly average and I've got the link—"

"To the research study that proves it, I know." She shot Marian a suspicious look as she peered into her nearly empty cocktail glass.

Marian gave Amy her full attention. "Sorry, I wasn't listening. Is this new woman going to upset the entire dating pool?"

"Well, I noticed her and I generally don't," Amy admitted.

"Better not," Hemma warned.

"Nobody compares to you, my love." Amy's hand slipped downward to cup Hemma's hip. "Let's go get our table, because I'm starved."

With a throaty laugh Hemma pressed her hip into Amy's hand. Her hand lovingly covered Amy's. "I know."

Marian blushed furiously. Ellie gave her a startled look.

Anything was better than the truth, Marian thought desperately. "Okay, I swiped some of your drink."

Ellie's indignation was sufficient to divert to safe topics, even if it was a recitation of the many burdens Ellie suffered being Marian's best friend. Marian let the various accustomed criticisms wash over her. Ellie had been her friend too long for it to have any sting, even when PMS made Marian certain the world could read her mind and every last secret. When dessert finally arrived, she lost herself in the chocolate cake. It was, after all, cheaper than therapy.

≈≈≈

Tuesday evening, June 3:

Bleeding, no. Cat vomit, yes. The vet says Trombone's got nerves. I'd like to puke on everyone who gives me nerves.

When I am reincarnated I want to come back as a lesbian's cat.

Had Amani's with Ellie who is dead set to land a new dyke in town. HER looked great tonight. Dinner Thursday. I-CARE on Saturday.

Jumping up and down has not made my period start. Tomorrow I am going to wear my new white shorts and not have a tampon on hand. It could work.

"So what's the deal, Trombone?" Marian scraped the last of the cat upchuck out of the heel of her favorite clogs. "Is it something I said?"

The tip of Trombone's tail moved just enough to agree.

"You smell Amani's on me, and I didn't bring you any, and then I ignored you to write in my journal, is that it? Hill, breathe someplace else." Marian pushed Professor Hill's snout the other direction. "Between your breath and Trombone's puke, it's aromatic enough in here."

Hill good-naturedly rolled over, covering the remainder of the small kitchen floor with his body and long collie tail.

"You're jealous of Hill's tail, aren't you, Trombone?" Sighing, Marian finished mucking out her shoe and poured her last glass of water for the day. She ought to have exercised.

Looking out the kitchen window into the backyard, she saw the sweep of headlights as Hemma and Amy pulled into the alley access behind their house.

"Make you a deal, body. You start bleeding and I'll start exercising." She snapped off the kitchen light on her way through to the tiny dining room she rarely used. Hill scurried out to the screened porch while Marian checked that the outer door was locked. Satisfied there were no intruders, Hill scampered past her knees to chase Trombone upstairs.

11

"Hill, you're just going to end up with a scratched nose!" Hill had yet to learn the politics of living with a cat. Marian locked the front door behind her and successfully avoided confronting the clutter in the living room by turning out the light. She'd clean next year, maybe.

Trombone, perched on the highest shelf of the tall bookcase at the top of the stairs, watched Marian thump her way up and ignored Hill's antic attempts to reach her. "You brought that creature into my house," the Russian Blue seemed to say, her tail wrapped tightly around her.

Marian paused as she did every night to touch her mother's quilt, which hung on the high wall of the stairwell. "When you pay the mortgage, my dear Trombone, you can decide who lives here. Hill won't be a puppy forever. He's only two. Another couple of years."

Trombone looked at the wall.

"Someday, Hill, you're going to bring that bookcase down on your head. Sit! Stay!" Marian held her finger inches from Hill's nose until he settled. "Oh, good boy! Good boy!"

Trombone's sigh was audible.

Marian paused a moment to regard the empty shelves. Their barren state was something she'd ignored successfully for some time. Well, it would be a place to put her textbooks. It felt weird to think of herself as a student again.

She brushed her teeth to the accompaniment of Hill's happy, going-to-bed panting. She knew that when she was nearly asleep Trombone would join them, taking, as usual, the center of the bed. It was genetically impossible for a cat to sleep anywhere else, especially if other beings wanted the bed as well.

Ordinary pajamas, she told herself. Some boxer shorts and a cotton tank—that's all that was called for on a warm summer night. It wasn't as if there was anyone to impress. No one had seen her in pajamas since Robyn, and Robyn hadn't liked her in pajamas. Robyn had preferred her—no, stop right there, she scolded herself. Robyn was a lying, cheating bitch of a destructive thief.

Cotton boxers and an equally soft tank was what the night called for, and that was all. Inner Slut pouted and whispered outrageous fantasies. I'm in control here, Marian thought weakly. I won't give in. But her hand passed over the comfortable cotton in the drawer, and reached instead for the sensuous silk of the nightshirt and boxer set that had never been designed for sleep.

She smoothed the thin black silk over her hips and couldn't quite look at herself in the mirror as she washed her face. She ignored the tingle down her spine that the cool fabric always triggered. With the lights out, moonlight spilled dimly through the open blinds of the spare room.

Close the blinds, she told herself. Close them, go to your room and get over it.

She sat down in the chair at the window. Count to twenty. If it's still dark in twenty, leave. Get over it.

The night was warm and heavy. Her body ached to be touched. Hormones, she told herself. You were even thinking about Ellie at dinner. It's just those stupid hormones making you this way.

She counted to a hundred twice, then soft light blossomed in the bedroom opposite where she sat.

Amy came to the window and pushed it half closed, then lowered the shade to match. There was a flash of aqua behind her, then the shade pressed against the glass. Two bodies, backlit by the bank of candles on their dresser, merged into one.

Don't do this, Marian told herself, even as she peered through the night. This is pathetic.

The aqua shirt floated to the floor. Two bare midriffs were visible as slacks were unzipped. It was easy to tell the slightly darker tone of Hemma's Middle Eastern skin from Amy's Irish paleness. Amy's hands on Hemma's waist.

Not Marian, but Amy lowering Hemma to the bed. Amy, stroking Hemma's back. Amy easing Hemma's bra from her shoulders. It was Amy's fingertips gently rousing Hemma's nipples to hard points of dusty rose and Amy's tongue teasing them further.

13

Amy and Hemma had a rhythm, a natural pace that spoke of ease and long practice, but it was never the same way twice. Some nights they were hurried, others languid. It could take minutes, or it could take hours.

Hemma had her hands in Amy's hair, pushing her down toward her hips. Amy resisted for a moment, said something. Hemma responded by opening her legs farther and tipping her hips up. Then it was Amy tasting Hemma. Marian swallowed hard and ached to feel the hot silk of Hemma's desire on her tongue. Hemma was frantic tonight, arching against Amy, exposing every inch of herself to Amy's seeking mouth.

Pathetic. Marian dashed away tears. How much of her life had she wasted wanting what she couldn't have?

Across the distance separating the two houses Marian could hear Hemma's moan. She had to close her eyes as she imagined that sound being one she had wrought. Her hands swept to her breasts, teasing her nipples through the thin fabric. Hormones . . . God, she wanted to be touched tonight. She imagined Hemma caressing her, whispering in her ear whatever magic she whispered to Amy, whatever promises that made Amy gasp for breath.

Hemma's sharp, low cry made her look again. Hemma wrapped her legs around Amy's hips, rising to meet her. Her face swam into Marian's feverish view. Beautiful with abandon, Hemma bit her lower lip, then her mouth curved with pleasure. Amy kissed her and they thrust together, inching their way across the bed. Amy was whispering in Hemma's ear and Hemma's moans sharpened to short cries of climax.

Marian gripped the sill, dizzied. She hated this feeling, and loved it. She told herself she wouldn't watch ever again but always did. Hemma's head hung off the bed, showing the elegant line of her throat, her lush breasts, her spread legs where Amy knelt. Bending over her, Amy said something low and urgent, then Hemma's rising wail flowed across the night, wrapping itself into the private places of Marian's heart.

Loving HER. Wanting HER. Days, weeks, years of wishing for something she would never have. Before Robyn, during Robyn, after Robyn, the ache never eased. Robyn had left two years ago after destroying everything that had mattered—except for Marian's heart. Hemma had always been and would always be the one who possessed it, whether she knew it or not.

She closed her eyes and pictured the perfect beach, the perfect sunset, the perfect woman by her side. One who could hold her, one who liked to be held. One who told her what was good about her more often than what was bad. She hungered for the velvet fullness of Hemma's lips against her skin.

Hemma's cries faded under Amy's deeper groans. Amy wouldn't stop until Hemma was taken care of. Wonderful Amy, tall, slender, intellectual, witty, all things that Marian envied. Amy gave Hemma everything she needed. Amy was a good lover, a good friend, and Hemma looked at Amy with stars in her eyes that never wavered.

Amy cried out as Hemma's nails raked over her back, then they were rolling over and Hemma, her face glowing with desire, pressed her hand between Amy's legs and watched her lover's every nuance of expression. She said something fiercely and Amy's loud, fervent, "Yes, baby, yes," was what Marian longed to say.

You're such a loser, she told herself. Go get laid, have a fling. She should make up a T-shirt for the I-CARE breakfast that screamed, "Forget the U-Haul, Just Fuck Me!"

She wiped away a tear. She'd feel better in a couple of days. She always felt better. She didn't have needs. She'd have dinner on Thursday and bask in Hemma's affection and Amy's friendship. It would be okay. Her hands swept over her breasts again, imagining the Hemma of her fantasies teasing her for hours. It was Hemma's hands that opened her thighs and touched her. She could hear Hemma's knowing laugh at what she found, and the low promise that all that heat, all that wet, would not go to waste.

Hemma's laughter drew her attention to the window again. Light but sultry, it accompanied the act of tossing a towel on the floor.

15

Spreading another on the bed, she pressed Amy down, straddling Amy's hips. She flowed up and down Amy's body, so sensual, so sexual, so captivating.

Marian could not stop watching and imagining, even knowing that it would never be her with Hemma. She should join Ellie in her dyke hunts. Practice whatever voodoo it was that got nearly every woman in town onto that couch of Carrie's. Move away, start a new life, move on.

Right. That would fix everything, she thought bitterly. She'd only let Robyn into her life and her bed as a cure for Hemma, and look where that had gotten her. Her unwilling gaze turned from the window to the box in the corner where the Robyn Ruins were sealed. Someday she would look inside again and maybe then her desire to commit murder would finally wane.

Tomorrow, she thought. I'll think about all of that tomorrow when I can't hear HER in my head. When I can't hear Robyn either.

She knew that tomorrow night she'd look in on Hemma's life again. The pain of not having Hemma's body was one she'd learned to bear. She could live without sex, yes, she could. It was harder to see them watch television with teacups on their stomachs, or argue fiercely about something in the newspaper, or read aloud to each other from books. Sex was easy. Robyn proved that. Intimacy, real intimacy, was something Marian had never known.

She wanted to make cornbread on cold nights and dash through the house naked for ice cream and spoons after sex. To lounge outside on a summer evening with only crickets for entertainment. To share the last piece of pie by passing the tin and a fork back and forth.

Amy was rolling Hemma across the bed. Hemma shrieked as they slipped off the edge where Marian could no longer see them. Their voices rose together in harmonic laughter.

2

"That's her."

Liddy Peel ignored the audible comment and pointed look directed at her. This town was too small, too humid, too hot, too provincial, and she hadn't even been here a week. Eight more weeks of this baking hell to go.

She was so fucking tired of being the fresh meat at the coffee-house market. She'd even heard that description of her whispered from one woman to another. Obviously, none of these cow town lightweights had seen the inside of a women's studies class. Not that her own foray into women's studies had turned out so well, but that was beside the fucking point. They were worse than men, she told herself, swear to freakin' god.

"Mocha, definitely with caffeine, on ice. With cream." The barely legal kid behind the counter mumbled an answer. So far they'd gotten it right, and the coffee was admittedly good.

At home she'd turn around now, check out who was in the place, on the off chance she would know someone. Not that it would have been likely, even in the student union. But she didn't know anybody here. She didn't want to know anybody here. The last thing she wanted was to make eye contact with one of the boa constrictors.

She couldn't go back to Cal, either. She was a graduate, finally. This job had come along at exactly the right moment in her life and she was lucky to have it.

She waited with her back to the rest of the long, narrow shop and the clusters of tables and groupings of sofas and easy chairs. To be fair, the Java House was as comfortable and collegiate as similar establishments in Berkeley. All it lacked was a plastic drum band outside. The radio was even tuned to the university station. Just like at home, she tried and failed to focus on what must be a vitally serious topic to engender such passion from the panelists. It sounded worthwhile, burning oat hulls instead of coal, but it just wasn't something she could get all worked up about.

Liddy edged sideways to make room for a shorter woman now ordering, who also wanted an iced mocha. They probably went through ice by the ton in the summer.

"Did you find what you needed about writing to the Queen of England?"

The oddity of the question made Liddy glance at the woman next to her, who was actually managing to hold a conversation with the taciturn boy. He was even smiling. Who knew?

Liddy took her mocha from him and added fake sugar and chocolate sprinkles. Her drink well-doctored she took a breath and turned to face the room. It was only about twenty feet to the door, but the most direct route took her past the boa constrictors. With relief, she detoured instead to the stack of *Daily Iowan* newspapers. Maybe somebody at the university was doing something remotely interesting this weekend.

She flipped it open to scan the headlines. Trailer-park residents were suing Coralville. All she knew about Coralville was that the city logo on the water tower was blue. A U of Iowa student was the first Iowan to reach the summit of Mt. Everest. The university was also proudly the home of a one-of-a-kind model lake, useful for numerous experiments.

One of the boa constrictors called out, "Marian! They've got brownies today."

"After the cake last night I really couldn't. Could I?"

Liddy wanted to roll her eyes. Lesbians and chocolate—what a cliché.

There was an abrupt silence and Liddy could feel the traded glances behind her back. The brunette with the overprocessed highlights whispered, "That's *her*. You were standing right next to her and you didn't say anything?"

The woman named Marian said in a normal tone, "Ellie, I'm quite sure she can hear every word you're saying."

Liddy stiffened her back and slowly turned around. "I may be new, but I'm not deaf."

Marian, at least, was looking her in the eye. "I'm sorry, I know what it's like. We were all new once."

An older woman with wedge-cut gray hair chimed in, "I'm the only native in the bunch."

"Oh hush, Terry, even you ended up on Carrie's holistic love couch," the brunette muttered. Her sharp brown gaze caught Liddy's for a moment and her smile grew conspiratorial. "You'll know Carrie when you see her."

Liddy didn't know whether to give vent to the indignation she felt at having her proclivities presumed, or to laugh, say something meaningless, and escape.

"It's okay," Marian said. "Ellie can't help herself."

Liddy found a tight smile. "Fortunately, I can."

Marian chortled appreciatively. "Good for you." She turned to the brunette again. "I have to get back to work, El. See you Friday night if not sooner."

Liddy headed for the door as well, not wanting to be drawn into any conversation with Ellie. She wasn't in the mood for sex. Maybe never again. She didn't need a girlfriend to be whole, and she didn't need sex to feel alive, swear to freakin' god.

She found herself following Marian down the wide Pedestrian Mall—what a *creative* name, she thought. The open-air mall was dotted with planters, benches and tables placed under broad, canopied trees. The smell of falafel and tahini sauce was evocative of home, and Liddy nearly got a pita just for comfort. But the coffee was refreshing enough.

The mall reached a dead end at a multistoried hotel, and, like Marian, she turned left, away from the fountain. She glanced longingly over her shoulder at the children running through the spray. To have no worries . . . sometimes being a grownup sucked. Liddy followed Marian past a massive play structure—deserted in the swelter of early afternoon—and around brightly painted construction barriers on South Linn. Marian turned into the large public library. Was that where she worked? Marian the Librarian? Swear to freakin' god, Liddy thought, this town is *small*.

It was a long walk to her rented house on North Dodge. Her cotton tank was a second skin by the end of the first block, but the iced mocha was wonderful going down. At least they took their coffee seriously.

The streets were shady and most of the yards brimmed with lush gardens, so as walks went, it didn't suck. What else would she do with her time?

Dating was out of the question. She was not interested in dating right now, and certainly not any of the predators at the coffeehouse.

It was annoying, being taken for granted. She'd been taken for granted by men before she'd realized she was a lesbian. Liking women did not make her see why she should stop being annoyed. She was wearing an old top and even older cutoffs. Her hair looked like she'd slept on it wet, which she had. And still the looks, the overt curiosity.

Maybe she screamed "sexy" and "dyke." She'd been told often that she did, so often it felt like an accusation, not a compliment. But she didn't think she damn well screamed "available for the asking," too. Swear to freakin' god, boobs made even lesbians stupid.

She was halfway home when she realized she'd forgotten to look for a store that sold candles. Telegraph Avenue at home would have offered a half-dozen street vendors, but here she'd have to make a bigger effort, obviously. The furnished house had a funky smell of mice and mothballs. Something with the aroma of the ocean would be relaxing and useful. It was a long, long way to the nearest tide. The house smelled old and dead and she was not either of those things, even if she felt like it sometimes.

She stopped walking for a moment, letting the waves of anger subside. She'd thought miles and fucking miles of fucking cornfields would be far enough away from the past. Far enough away that she'd stop being mad and hurt and crushed. That she'd start feeling like she could smile and not cry.

She needed to destroy something but lacked a viable target. If Jerry Falwell had appeared in front of her right then she'd have cheerfully dismembered him and then beat his fascist cronies to death with his bones.

What are you doing in Iowa fucking City, Liddy? She pressed one hand over her eyes and took a long, steadying breath. To do a job, she reminded herself. If she did it well it could be a good future. Swear to freakin' god, she was not going to be thirty and still wondering what she wanted to be when she grew up.

She trudged up the driveway of her temporary home. The living room of the house was Iowa City rental chic. What matched was broken while the ugliest furniture would survive the apocalypse, forever pristine. Rates were low for summer and the lease was up July 31 when students would flood the town again. By then Liddy hoped to be home in Berkeley, where she belonged, her laptop overflowing with notes and citations.

She snapped on the boombox. Groove Armada oozed over the tick of a single clock and the drone of traffic on the busy street outside. Oatmeal and bananas for dinner?

She dialed up her voicemail out of habit and flinched at the sound of her mother's amplified voice.

"Daddy and I are just wondering how you are. Have you looked up my cousin Selma yet? Cedar Rapids is only thirty-five miles. You take the interstate—"

She punched ahead thirty seconds.

"Then you turn left onto Runnymede. Daddy can send you the map if you need it. Are you eating something more than oatmeal? We love you, honey. Call when you get the chance."

It was her first and only message since her arrival four days ago, so she saved it. She could listen again later and pretend she actually had a reason for voice mail.

She was only a few steps from the phone when it chirped. She snatched up the handset.

"This is Faye with University Library Services. I'm calling to let you know that eight of the nine texts you requested have arrived. They'll be held under your name for the next four days."

"Oh." Liddy was at a loss for words. "You actually called."

"We always do, as you should have been informed—"

"It's okay. Nobody's ever called before, that's all."

"Really? But it's our policy. Never?"

"Oh, I'm new. Nobody at home ever called, I mean. In California."

"Oh, I see." Incredulity changed to understanding. There was even a nuance of pity in the librarian's voice.

"How late are you open tonight?"

"Until eight on Wednesdays."

"Great." She could grab the books, get some dinner out for a change. Then come home and settle in to read something useful.

The rest of the day no longer seemed so bleak. At least she would get some work done toward claiming that first paycheck. She was here to work.

❧

She'd had her doubts that the in-window air conditioning unit had any effect at all until she stepped outside just after seven. The humidity descended on her shoulders like a blanket and sweat instantly prickled the length of her back.

She stood in the shade of the house for minute, glaring at the Hummer. It had been fun to drive across country. She'd slept in it three nights in Wal-Mart parking lots. She'd cruised past big rigs and RVs on steep grades.

It barely fit in the narrow two-track cement driveway, and there was no street parking. And it got thirteen miles to the gallon, if she was lucky.

Leave it to her absentee biological father to make a gesture like this: lavish, conspicuous, yet undeniably fun. He wanted her to love the outdoors the way he did, routinely ignoring the fact that she was a city girl down to the tips of her pink-tinted toenails. The insurance was astronomical and there were times when she couldn't afford to fill the thirty-two gallon tank. It was not the vehicle of a Master in History with no firm job prospects.

Her mother, when she'd seen it, had simply said, "How typical of Jim." Liddy heard every bounced child-support check in her mother's sigh.

Daddy, her mother's second husband, had helped her explore all its little gadgets, then advised her to sell it and pay off her student loans.

She steeled herself for the tight squeeze through the fence posts at the base of the driveway. A scratch would probably cost a thousand bucks to repair. Her biological father was there at the major birthdays and events like college graduation, but not around for the little things. He never had been. Jason and Jeanine, being older, were long used to asking him for stuff, but she had never felt enough like his daughter to do that. She'd been two months old when her mother had filed for divorce.

She had the behemoth halfway out of the driveway when the next spate of traffic reached her. Aware she was holding up the busy street, she continued inching out and told herself she could do this every day. She would not sell her car just because it was too big for Iowa fucking City. She was only here for the summer.

Nobody honked, but she felt as if gun sights were focused on her California license plates.

Free at last, she headed toward campus, narrowly avoiding a head-on with a bus. The streets were too narrow.

She managed to find two adjacent parking spaces in the lot next to the university's main library. She jammed a Cal Bears cap over her hair, pulled her ponytail through the back and welcomed the cool interior.

Her reserved books were located and checked out to her with alacrity. Scanning the bibliography of the first book she saw several items she ought to look for. Wandering through the musty stacks she felt calm again. Libraries had that effect on her.

She was startled when the lights flickered. A glance at her watch told her it was nearly eight. She took her new list of needed texts to the research desk. At least the lines were short. She'd be spoiled when she got home to Cal again. Stop that, she thought. You're not a Cal student any longer, remember?

"This one I can't help you with. It's out to a professor and they can keep a book indefinitely." The slightly swishy reference librarian seemed genuinely regretful. "Technically they have to bring it back, but short of us sending a security guard to their office, we can't really force the issue."

"Oh, well, dang. I saw in the catalog it's the only copy."

"Try the P.L. They have a lot of general medical reference."

"P.L.?"

"Public library. It's just off the Ped Mall."

"Oh, really? Yeah, I guess it's worth stopping in." She remembered now Marian the Librarian turning into the sizable building.

"Plus they have fiction and videos."

"There's an idea." Liddy thanked him for the advice, checked out the three additional books she'd decided on, and headed into the sunset swelter.

Parking the Hummer near the Pedestrian Mall was another chore. Maybe she should settle her student loans and buy something more practical. One of those hybrids that would get her home to California on one tank of gas, maybe. Or a nice Jeep. A Jeep could be fun and practical. Of course it would never double as a moving van. The Hummer had held a ton of crap and left plenty of room for sleeping, even if one morning she'd woken up with the winch in her back.

Standing in the nonfiction area, she realized her reference number for the text was the Library of Congress method and of course the public library used the Dewey Decimal System. There were no terminals free to look it up again and suddenly the rows seemed very long. She could guess roughly where the book ought to be, but sharp hunger pangs were making it hard to think.

She knew closing time had to be fast approaching. Discouraged, she almost left, but her roaming glance caught sight of a sign for the reference desk. The librarians would have their own terminals.

The woman at the desk was huddled over something as Liddy approached, but she abruptly looked up. Oh, Liddy thought in surprise. Marian again.

"May I help you find a resource?"

If Marian recognized her it didn't show. "I have a Library of Congress number for something I need," she began hesitantly.

"The title is good enough. Allow me to look up the shelf location for you, if we have it." Marian took the proffered paper and tapped rapidly on her keyboard. "We do, and I show it on the shelf. And this . . ." She wrote a number series neatly on the paper. "This is your call number."

Encouraged, Liddy refused the businesslike offer to help her find it, and hurried away after pleased thanks. She thumbed through the book quickly. Yes, it would be useful. Great bibliography on women and medical ethics, too. Her employer was bound to be interested in that topic.

Marian the Librarian smiled pleasantly when Liddy returned. "Did you find everything you were interested in?"

"Yes, thank you. I don't have a library card, though."

"No problem. Do you have a valid driver's license?"

"Yes, but California." She dug in her pocket.

"As long as it's current. You need a local address, even if it's temporary. Here's the form. Do you need a pen?"

"Nope." She flipped open her little billfold that held her license and credit card.

Marian glanced at the license, then said, "Actually, I'm not the one to show that to. When you've completed the form you can take it to the circulation desk and they'll give you the card and check out the book to you. That's when you'll need your ID."

"How long can I have this book for, do you know?"

"Two renewals for four weeks can be completed online as long as it hasn't been reserved by someone else. And I'm pretty sure this one won't be in high demand. The total time, therefore, would be twelve weeks, including the initial checkout period."

Liddy blinked, not used to such ready information so clearly provided. "That will cover my stay here, thank you." She felt awkward, for just a moment, as if she should acknowledge their earlier meeting. Finally, she gestured a wave with the book.

"Happy reading." Marian looked behind Liddy. "May I help you find a resource?"

"I'm still looking for a phone number in Dallas."

As she walked toward the checkout area Liddy was aware of the measured, patient tone of Marian's voice, completely at odds with the rude edge of the woman she was helping.

There was not enough money on the planet to make her work with the public, Liddy thought. Swear to freakin' god.

She was out on the sidewalk before she identified a slight annoyance that Marian the Librarian had not shown any sign she'd recognized Liddy. She was tired of being ogled, true. But she was not used to being forgotten.

She didn't want to go home, not yet. Plus she was starving. She dropped the book at the Hummer and walked down the mall to

Prairie Lights Bookstore. They had great muffins in the café and creative protein drinks, too. The boa constrictors seemed to prefer the Java House, so she was likely not going to be accosted at the bookstore. Like libraries, bookstores were places she could lose all track of time. She'd grab a muffin and java, then browse.

To her dismay she hadn't even reached the top of the first flight of stairs when she heard, "That's *her*."

"God, Amy was right."

Fuck. Fuck and fuck it, she was not going to be hit on. Not in a bookstore. The first and last time she'd let that happen had turned out badly. It was why she wasn't in California this summer.

She turned tail and went back out onto the darkening street, nearly knocking into a plump blonde. "Sorry."

"It's okay, no harm done." At least the woman's smile wasn't predatory. Nothing like . . . "Excuse me."

Liddy realized she was blocking the doorway. "Sorry."

"Blessed be." With a nod the blonde went into the store. Liddy let the door swing shut behind her.

When she heard the door reopen and then that woman Ellie's unmistakable Midwest twang, she accelerated toward the cover of the trees and shops. There had been a candle and perfume store marked in the online tourist map. It might still be open. She bolted the length of one block and skittered around the corner at the fountain.

She was in luck. Sandalwood wafted into the damp night from Soap Opera's open door. Liddy greeted the clerk and turned her attention to the vast array of candles. Something that smelled like the ocean would be perfect.

After a half-dozen sniffs of different varieties she could no longer tell one from another. She went with "Landward Breeze" because it didn't make her nose itch, then a bottle of rosemary and ginger body wash seemed exactly what she needed. At the checkout counter, she snagged a bag of lavender potpourri.

The pale teenager at the register abruptly came to life. "We're having a special on our homemade musk. A free infusion if you spend twenty-five dollars. Would you like to test it?"

Liddy shrugged and leaned over the open vial for a sniff. It was too much. She recoiled and shook her head vehemently. "No, not for me."

The clerk gave her an odd look as she rung up the purchases. Not quickly enough Liddy escaped into the twilight.

That scent . . . She had never, ever wanted to smell it again. Not in her hair, her sheets, her pillows. Not in the closet, in a drawer, unexpectedly inside a jacket. That scent . . . Holy shit, she hated it. To her horror, she felt a treacherous throb between her legs, and visions tortured her, reminded her of how she had been with that scent filling her head.

She realized she was nearly running, even though there were no demons here to pursue her. That was why she was two thousand fucking miles from home. Nothing here was supposed to remind her of . . . that lying, manipulative bitch.

Nearly blind with anger and heartbreak, she stumbled to a stop in the parking lot near the library. Shaking, she put one hand on a nearby wall. The brick surface was still warm to the touch.

The night was humid and sticky. Home was so far away.

She wanted to kill something. Someone.

She slapped the brick with her open palm, but it wasn't enough. With a gasp, she leapt into self-defense stance, then without hesitation twirled into a roundhouse kick. The sole of her Teva made a satisfying thud against the wall. Again.

Again.

That bitch had to get out of her head sometime.

"R," she said under her breath in time with her next kick. More letters for every kick, trying to obliterate the name that went with the memory of that smell. She wanted to stomp out the image cut into her brain of the woman with the cheap smile and empty soul. Robyn fucking Vaughn, that bitch.

3

Wide-eyed, Marian stood at the back corner of the library, transfixed by the sight of the woman Ellie called Fresh Meat kicking the hell out of the building.

It was mesmerizing.

Such precision and skill, and clearly a great deal of rage. She was chanting something as she kicked, as if it were a ritual of purification.

Careful not to disturb the angry, focused woman, Marian made her way down the Ped Mall toward the Java House. A second coffee would be overindulgent, but today it was medicinal. When the rhythmic thumping abruptly ceased, she turned to check that everything was okay. All she saw was the departing back of the mystery woman disappearing into the falling dark. Wow. Not that she was quite such a mystery any longer, however.

Rounding the corner, she saw the line at the Java House was out the door. Damn, another block to Prairie Lights, then. It was smaller, but often less crowded. She crossed the street, wilting at the heat rising from the asphalt. Perspiring more than she liked, Marian hurried up the stairs to the bookstore's café, eager for a decaf mocha to end the longest Wednesday of her life.

"Marian!"

She waved to Carrie and Jersey, and realized once she was in the line that Terry was waiting at the counter for her order. Good, she'd have some pleasant conversation to take her mind off her wretched day.

Terry lifted her heavy gray hair off her neck. "Hot enough for ya?"

"It'll be worse." Marian broke into a grin. "August."

"I've had animals with heat stroke all week. It's good for business, but honestly, how hard is it to remember to water your pets?" Terry thanked the server for the drinks and headed back to the table where Jersey was waiting.

"Did you find her, Ellie?" Carrie sounded highly amused.

Marian glanced over her shoulder. Ellie was panting and looking uncustomarily disheveled.

"That was aerobic. I don't think I've ever seen you run that fast." Jersey kicked a chair in Ellie's direction.

Ellie collapsed into the chair. "Not a sign of her. I have no idea where she disappeared to."

"She took one look at you and ran," Terry observed as she set one of her two froth-topped cups in front of Jersey.

"She didn't even see me." Ellie mopped her forehead with a napkin.

"Well, she was definitely running from something, dear." Carrie got up for more chocolate sprinkles. "She nearly knocked me over. I barely had a chance to wish her blessed be and she was off."

"Amy was right, wasn't she?" Ellie clicked her tongue, making Marian stare at the ceiling.

"A lovely woman," Carrie agreed. "Doesn't anyone have a name?"

"Lovely? That's an understatement. And believe me, if I had found her out there I'd have gotten a name. And thanks for not eating my frozen yogurt while I was gone, guys. Good thing Marian wasn't here—she'd have finished it."

"Thanks, Ellie, I love you, too." Marian ordered her frozen decaf mocha with skim, no cream, and sauntered back to the table to drop off her backpack.

"Wouldn't you say so, Marian? That new woman—she's not just lovely. Talk about Femme on a Triscuit." Ellie licked the back of her spoon suggestively.

"She's quite attractive. I hope we're not going to argue about that for the next hour." She wondered what Ellie would think of the building assault Marian had witnessed. Edible yes, Inner Slut agreed enthusiastically, with those slender legs emerging from those tiny red shorts with the slits on the side.

Shut up, Marian thought. Edible, maybe, but a tetch unstable. She opened her mouth to say something but stopped. It had been odd, but also, well, private.

"Those eyes," Ellie moaned. "I don't think I've ever seen eyes like that. A sort of creamy blue with hints of green."

Terry twisted the tiny gold hoop in her left ear. "Where do you suppose she gets that skin from?"

Jersey smacked Terry lightly on the shoulder. "Honey, as if how she looks concerns you."

"I've got eyes," Terry said mildly.

"I thought you only had eyes for me."

"I do when it counts, sweetie." Terry abruptly frowned. "Do you think if I tried I could be covered in more pet hair?"

"Hazards of being a vet, honey. Good thing I'm not allergic." Jersey made a face at her drink. "It's not like any of you looked higher than her shoulders."

"I looked at her eyes," Ellie protested. "Eventually."

Marian wandered back to the counter for her last indulgence of the day. More chocolate on top and two packets of fake sugar completed it to her satisfaction.

Terry scooted over one chair to give Marian easier access to the table.

"New software on the library terminals," Marian said.

"You've had a stinky day, then." Ellie raised her mug for a clink of solidarity.

"Another understatement. It's easy to use but General Public and all the Lieutenants don't like change." The first hit of coffee, chocolate and melting ice felt like ambrosia on her tongue. She was going to live.

"I couldn't work with the public," Jersey volunteered. "I don't know how you do it."

"I like my job, even though today I wanted to commit multiple homicides. I like helping people find what they want." It was hard to explain, though she'd tried before. "Most people want to Blue Book their car or get the latest bestseller, but sometimes what they really want is information about a dream they cherish. Like information about an exotic holiday spot. Or how to file a patent application."

Jersey shrugged. "But can't they use a computer to find books these days?"

There was a short silence. Any other day of the entire month and Marian would not have been offended by Jersey's usual lack of tact. She wanted to snap back that search words were an art to choose, and one of the real pleasures of her job.

"Oh. I did it again, huh? Sorry, Marian. I know a computer could not possibly do your job, I know that. I was just thinking it would be nice if most people could do self-help and let you do the harder searches."

Mollified, Marian smiled. "I understand what you mean."

"Which is a good thing," Ellie said. "Because she's got PMS."

Terry made a show of inching away from Marian. "Do I need asbestos gloves?"

"Your hormone swings used to be worse than mine, and you know it."

"Thankfully, I am largely free of such worries these days. I love being fifty. Fifty plus lube equals fun."

"Terry!" Jersey flushed. "Do you have to tell our secrets?"

Terry got the wicked smile that Marian loved. "Yes, it's the liberation of my inner crone."

"Marian, dear, have you tried that preparation I gave you for your hormone fluctuations?" Carrie regarded Marian serenely.

"It doesn't seem to make much difference. I either want to murder strangers or commit chocolate suicide."

"Oh, dear. Perhaps you should stop by and we'll work out something else."

Marian fought down a blush, remembering the first time she'd stopped into Carrie's herb shop. Right now, her hormones raging, that night with Carrie ran through her mind like a DVD pausing at just the good parts.

Ellie nudged Marian, probably all too aware of what Marian was thinking. Damn, then she did blush and everyone, including Carrie, snickered.

Inner Historian reported that, according to the Iowa City dance card she carefully maintained in her memory banks, everyone at the table had been with Carrie at least once. Marian wasn't sure anyone at the table besides Carrie knew it as well. It was an odd feeling, realizing Carrie knew what they all sounded like when they climaxed. Well, she guessed they had all climaxed. She knew she had. Twice. Carrie's knowledge of female anatomy was better than some of the gynecologists she'd been to.

Now that she thought about it, she realized they all knew what Carrie sounded like, too. It felt, well, naughty, if she pondered it too long. Inner Prude suggested that it would probably be wise, then, not to think about it. Inner Slut, however, wanted to dwell on all the details. Useless hormones.

"Hey, Patty!" Ellie had the best view of the door, Marian realized, because it was several seconds before Patty's short black hair and broad shoulders came into her line of sight.

"Can't stay," Patty called back. "Just grabbing a latte for Wen. The line at the Java House was out the door."

"I'm just wiped out," Marian said. She allowed Inner Slut to watch Patty taking up her position in line. Even standing still Patty's muscles rippled. "I'm going to drink this, go home and sleep until noon."

"Since when do you get Thursdays off?" Ellie demanded. "I've got more pipes to rip out."

"I don't, but I might call in queer. I feel really crappy."

Carrie said kindly, as usual, "A good herbal tea would help, I'm sure."

"Tea is not what Marian needs." Ellie sighed. "If I don't get the new woman, Marian should. She's overdue."

"I'm not in the market," Marian muttered. She clamped her mouth shut. Damned hormones. She'd almost blurted out she was in love with her next-door neighbor. Something in her belly felt suddenly off and a dull throb thudded against her pelvic bone.

"You ought to be." Terry gave her a philosophical look. "Don't waste your thirties. Mine were fun, but too short."

"She was in today." The throb repeated itself.

Everyone paused and Marian realized what she'd said.

"What's her name?" Ellie smiled sweetly, which meant she was resisting the urge to smack Marian.

"I'm sorry, that's library records."

Jersey set down her cup and gave Marian an intent stare. "Oh, not her name, surely."

"Yes, including her name. And don't call me Shirley."

"Marian, how long have we been friends?"

"Forever, Ellie, and I still can't tell you." At the moment, Marian honestly couldn't remember. The throb in her pelvis was getting stronger.

"I'll never forgive you if Sandy gets her first."

"Join the F.B.I. and bring some special agents with you invoking the Patriot Act, and then I can tell you."

"She lives here in town?"

"I can't tell you that."

"Marian!"

"Ellie!"

Ellie got that look, that about-to-burst-into-song look.

"Ellie, don't you dare. Not today."

"Tell me her name."

Patty paused at the table, leaning her square, buff frame over Ellie's shoulder. "If you sing 'Marian the Librarian' I will help Marian kill you."

"Amen," Carrie added. "Fresh Meat is not worth fighting over."

"Oh, I don't know, she's gorgeous." Ellie continued to give Marian a narrow stare.

"Let's do a pool." Terry smiled brightly. "I'm willing to place a bet."

"Oh no, guys, please . . ." Marian began. She suddenly ached all over. She was in no mood for proof that everyone regarded her as the least likely to attract the interest of a new woman. That she didn't want to attract anyone at this point in her life was suddenly beside the point.

Dollar bills floated onto the table. Even Patty dropped one in.

"My money's on Carrie," Jersey said firmly.

"How flattering—but our auras weren't compatible." Carrie regarded Marian serenely. "I'm not seeking her out."

"Neither am I," Marian said quickly. "And I'm not betting."

"We should get Hemma and Amy to bet," Terry added.

Great, just what I need, Marian thought, the woman I love betting for or against me seducing someone else. Her mood went from charcoal to black.

"So everyone is backing Ellie?" Terry poised her pen over a napkin she'd already dated. "You want to change your mind, honey?"

Jersey glanced at Carrie and then nodded. "Okay, I'll back Ellie, too."

"Wait." Ellie put her hand over the small pile of bills. "If you all pick me you'll just get your money back. This is pointless."

"Then I'll make it interesting," Carrie said. "I'm betting on Marian."

"But I'm not trying."

Terry did her perfect Yoda impression. "There is no try, only do, young Skywalker."

"But I don't want to do her." Marian glanced around. "Seriously."

"There are lots of babies in the world that prove you don't have to be actively trying to create something new." Carrie shrugged. "It'll make the bet worth doing."

"Guys?" Marian put her hand on her abdomen.

"What?" Ellie snapped.

"I've got cramps."

The napkins on the table ruffled in the collective sigh of relief.

Ellie touched her cup to Marian's in salute. "Thank goodness."

"Way to go." Terry slapped Marian on the shoulder. She gathered up the bills and folded them into the napkin on which she had recorded their bets. "Carrie takes the long odds, so we have ourselves a horse race."

"I'm not mounting up," Marian muttered.

"This is the most politically incorrect thing I've done in ages," Carrie said. She shook a wrinkle out of her long cotton dress. "Gaia works in mysterious ways, however."

"It's okay," Marian said. "Everything will be okay now." She smiled, feeling serene for the first time in days. Then she recalled that she was wearing her new white cargo shorts. Typical, just typical. "See y'all Friday night."

Wednesday evening, June 4

Feel better. Very settled now that I've made up my mind on the M.L.S. It helps not to be hormonal. I wish that the whole bleeding thing had an opt-out choice.

School is going to upset my routine in the fall, but I hope not Thursday night dinner. It's the one thing I know I can look forward to every week.

Trombone chose the mocs today and Hill burped up more cotton. I should just pick up new underwear every time I go to the store. Maybe if I tell

Trombone that my old boots are my absolute favorite shoes she'll choose them for her hairball gifts. Ellie has the short odds to land the new woman. Best of luck to her.

Looking forward to telling HER and Amy tomorrow night about the M.L.S. HER will be pleased I've taken this step.

❧

"First, click the 'Reset to New User' button," Marian said, trying hard not to sound as if she'd already said it a hundred times so far today. She had really wanted to call in sick except Eric would have skinned her alive for leaving him with Bill *and* new software to show every user. "After you log on, the timer will start over. It's designed to help remind people that others might be waiting to use the Internet. And this button here will turn off the Internet filters."

At least this patron appeared to have the basic skills to navigate the new software. The older woman peered up at Marian over her glasses. "I don't disagree that it is useful to have a way to make access to the computers more fair, but I'm not comfortable with anyone being able to know what I've been looking up while I'm here."

Marian agreed with the patron's concern. "If you log out properly, the system will purge your user history for this session."

The patron two computers down asked, "But what if I want to come back to a site again? I don't have anything to hide."

The woman bristled. "Neither do I, but that doesn't mean I don't want to preserve my privacy. I'm planning a trip to Cairo and somebody could decide I'm a terrorist!"

Marian said soothingly, "As a system, our library has decided that the patron's privacy is more important than the convenience of bookmarks and even being able to look up books you've checked out in the past. Amazon.com knows more about your reading preferences than we ever will." Marian did not want to get into a debate about the USA Patriot Act, at least not right now. She doubted either patron cared that significant federal funds would be withheld if the Internet filters weren't defaulted to On at every workstation. "What we don't know we can't be compelled to tell."

37

Neither patron seemed particularly mollified, but they went back to their browsing and Marian returned to her shared stint at reshelving. It was such a bitch when the circulation clerks were collectively unreliable. The usually steady Toni had been out sick a lot lately, too, and with students gone for the summer it was difficult to find substitutes.

Eric emerged from smallest of the three study rooms, smiling pleasantly at the latest job applicant. Even from across the floor, Marian could see he wasn't impressed. Mary Jane, the library manager, likewise had that stiff what-a-waste-of-time look that had taken Marian two years to learn to read.

After the applicant had left, Marian joined them. "Let me guess. She wants to be a librarian because of the serene quiet and getting to read books all day."

"And she thinks working with the public will be fun." Eric sighed heavily.

"She obviously hasn't before," Marian muttered. "Sorry. I just hate to see another wide-eyed librarian hopeful crushed by reality."

Mary Jane pushed her glasses into position. "It's not a career for the weak-at-heart. Thank you, Eric. Marian, you sit in on the next one at two."

Marian trailed after Mary Jane into her office. "I've made up my mind. I'm going to do it."

"Have you?" Mary Jane beamed. "I think it's an excellent decision. Make some capital off that master's in history you went to such trouble to get."

Marian basked in Mary Jane's approval. She was both friend and mentor. "I'll have that recommendation letter for you to sign some time next week. The application isn't due for the fall semester until then."

"So I'll have another Master of Library and Information Science working for me who'll want a promotion." Mary Jane arched an eyebrow. "Might even be after my job."

"I would never do that—oh. You are such a tease."

Mary Jane's neutral expression didn't alter. "So I've been told."

"By whom?"

"Don't be impertinent."

Marian went back to the book carts with a giggle in her throat. Mary Jane could give off that reserved, cool, asexual vibe all she wanted, but Marian had seen her in her leathers.

A voice rose from the direction of the reference desk. "You must be kidding!"

Marian peered through the shelving to see what the problem was. Oh, now that was poetic justice. Bill, the lazy lizard, was the recipient of Seventh Dimension Bitch's current frustration. They deserved each other. Let Bill show her how to use the new software.

She was shelving a volume on medical politics when she remembered the book Fresh Meat—really, she scolded herself, you can't call her that—had needed yesterday. She'd probably like this one as well. Libby Peel, she recalled, from her hurried glance at the woman's license. If Peel came in again, Marian would point the book out. Reader advisories in nonfiction were her specialty. She didn't want to be a library manager like Mary Jane—too many stressful administrative details, not to mention having to always be poised, cool and more dressed up. Library managers did not get to gad about in shorts and tank tops when it was ninety. A collection manager, now that had appeal. She could debate collection development policy all day and go back after dinner for more.

Getting her M.L.S. was the right thing to do. Besides, she had the time to do it. She ought to have done it when Robyn left. If she had, she'd be done now.

The bridge has seen that water, as Gran always said. She would start this fall and in two years be done.

There, she told herself. You've taken control of your life. Remember to stop at Hy-Vee on the way home for cream and everything will be fine.

❧

Marian lifted the saucepan off the burner just as the sugar and water turned golden. She drizzled the syrup into her favorite baking dish for custard and coated the inside carefully. Hemma loved Marian's flan, and the key was in the caramel.

Marian always brought dessert because Hemma loved sweets. She said she could avoid most other temptations, knowing every week she'd get to sample one of Marian's delicacies.

That first dinner, the first time they'd invited her over after she'd moved in next door . . . the very first dinner had set the pattern of the last seven years. Hemma loved sweets, and Marian loved Hemma's smile. She'd do anything for it.

Cracking eggs into her favorite mixing bowl made her briefly wonder how many eggs she'd broken over the years for Hemma's sweet tooth. However many it was, it was worth it.

She beat the eggs absent-mindedly. When making dessert for their dinners together she always relived the day six years ago she had realized she was in love with Hemma. It was a cherished memory, one that comforted her while she worked alone in her kitchen.

They'd been to an estate sale out near the Amana Colonies, spending hours sorting through boxes looking for treasure. Amy had no patience for it, so she'd stayed home and was warming up the grill for their return.

"Here," Hemma had said. "This is you."

Marian looked down at the slender book with the slightly stained cover. "*Francie to the Rescue?*"

Hemma had her head back under a table, sorting through boxes. "For your collection."

"I have a collection?"

Hemma sat back on her haunches to laugh at Marian. "You don't realize you have a collection of girl books?"

"I hadn't thought about it. I just like them. I don't know this series."

"Hey—look at this! There's a whole box!" Hemma hauled the container out from under the table. "Those girls who fly their air-

40

planes about the country looking for adventures? Those books are here."

It was treasure of the first order. Marian dropped to the floor next to Hemma. "Wow. I wonder if I can afford them?"

Hemma put her hand briefly on top of Marian's. "How can you *not* afford them? This is you."

She blinked into Hemma's eyes, those startling black eyes. She knows me, Marian thought. She looks at me, and knows me.

She studied the contents of the box, aware that she was blushing as she always did over the slightest thing. Hemma was chattering about the quality of the books, which was fair for 1920 editions. All Marian could think about was how much she wanted to kiss Hemma.

In something of a daze, she bought the lot for less than she thought. At home, Hemma excitedly helped her arrange them in order of publication. Her dining room table was covered.

"This is a collection. You can't deny it. The Nancy Drews are going to fill up what's left of the shelf in your study. You're going to need a new bookcase."

Coming out of the kitchen, Marian paused with the two glasses of iced tea. She actually felt something tremble between her legs, a sensation so unexpected and sharp she had to set the glasses down on the side bar. Hemma stood with her back to Marian, hands on her jean-clad hips, and all Marian wanted to do was put her arms around Hemma from behind.

Put her arms around her and touch. Soft, womanly stomach, lush breasts, angular shoulders . . . she wanted to bury her face in the dark twist of hair at the nape of Hemma's neck, and kiss her shoulders, turn her around and kiss her mouth. Fall to the floor and be kissed.

She knew her face was flaming red.

Hormones, she thought. Too long since Carrie. Carrie and she had been only one night, too, shortly after Marian had moved to Iowa City from Chicago. Before that . . . too long. These waves of feeling for Hemma are just lust, she told herself vehemently, and you need to get over it or you'll lose her as a friend.

She watched Hemma skip across her backyard to be folded into Amy's arms. All through their outdoor dinner under the arbor they'd all built together earlier in the summer, Marian wondered if she had a chance, but the truth was undeniable. Everything Hemma was became *more* whenever she looked at Amy. Hemma without Amy would not be the Hemma she was falling in love with. Separately, they were complete women and distinct in their personalities. When they sat side-by-side it was as if they blurred around their edges.

Falling in love—she didn't know the feeling until it washed over her like the scent of Hemma's beloved climbing jasmine, heady and inescapable. She wanted somehow to be what Amy was to Hemma, to be the one who made her glow with joy. But she had to face facts. Amy was everything Hemma loved. Hemma had a Ph.D., and so did Amy, and they both taught at the university. Her own master's in history had prepared her for a career as a data entry clerk.

"That's really what you ought to do." Hemma passed her the platter of ribs.

"Sorry, I was thinking about the books and where I'll put them," Marian lied. Would she ever stop blushing?

"You could put a bookcase at the top of the stairs," Amy suggested. "I know a couple of women who build them, if you wanted something custom-sized."

"Thanks, I'll think about it." Though Marian had no idea how a professor of rhetoric got around so much, Amy always knew somebody who could build, fix, create, drywall, plan, plumb or hammer whatever needed it. Her best friend Ellie was kept pretty busy moonlighting with plumbing jobs just from Amy's word-of-mouth referrals.

"Anyway," Hemma continued, "you're wasted doing data entry for the med center. I know it pays decent enough."

"It's not like I can do anything with my history master's. I really don't want a Ph.D. Teaching's not my thing, anyway. I don't have the patience."

"Librarian—you should be a librarian. You'd get to read books all day."

Amy chortled. "I don't think it works that way, my love. Have you ever seen a librarian actually reading?"

Marian said slowly, "I've rarely seen librarians with an open book." The table seemed to shimmer in the afternoon sunlight. Something is happening, she thought, as if the world just took a left turn. Common sense cautioned that the career path for a librarian was surely a dead end professionally and monetarily. But data entry wasn't?

"You should look into it." Hemma relieved Marian of the basket of cornbread they'd picked up at their favorite Amana Colony bakery. "Though it occurs to me that you'd be Marian the Librarian from River City."

Marian felt as if a breeze would blow her away. "Maybe I should watch the musical again so I'm prepared for the jokes."

"How about tonight?"

Amy groaned. "We watched that insipid Lifetime movie last week. I don't think I can take *The Music Man* this week."

Hemma touched her arm and Marian thought she would melt. Melt not from the heat, but from the tenderness. "Are you okay?"

"I've always hung out at the library. I love books, I love *finding* books. It always seemed like whatever I could dream I could find at the library. And ever since I was a girl I thought librarians were the guardians of all the mysteries of time. It never occurred to me . . ."

She had to be crimson by now, but Hemma was smiling at her so encouragingly. "What never occurred to you?"

"That I could be one of the guardians."

Hemma arched an eyebrow and for one of those rare moments over the course of the last seven years, the universe had seemed made up of just the two of them. "This is you."

All these years later, Marian had to acknowledge, Hemma still saw her for who she was.

She checked the doneness of the custard and inhaled the rich, creamy aroma. Hemma's favorite dessert was perfect to celebrate the day Marian had decided to go all the way with her career as a librarian.

An M.L.S. combined with her hitherto useless history degree and her years of experience could net her a job in collection development and perhaps eventually the management of a specialized historical collection. Even being a library manager—administrative headaches and all—had a certain appeal.

She really would be a guardian then, a keeper of dreams. Hemma had shown her that she could have that future. It was a gift and she would always love Hemma for it.

"What *is* that? It smells divine!" Hemma took the covered pan from Marian and sniffed again. "Flan?"

"Chocolate almond flan, and still warm the way you like it."

"You are the most wonderful woman." Hemma hurried to the kitchen. "The pasties are just about done."

"Pasties!" Marian worried abruptly that she'd forgotten it was a special occasion. Pasties were her favorite, her absolute favorite.

Amy came skipping down the stairs. "Heya. And hamburger milk gravy."

"Oh, what have I done to deserve this?"

Amy skittered to a stop halfway across the living room. "Forgot something. I'll be right back down." Marian continued through the house to the kitchen.

Hemma was flushed as she lifted a cookie sheet from the oven. "They're done."

"Done and perfect," Marian breathed. The half-moon pockets were golden on top and brown at the edges. The savory aroma of shredded beef, onions and potatoes made her feel a bit faint. "My pie crust will never be as good as yours no matter how much you try to teach me."

Hemma's back was to her when she answered. "You make great pies."

"They'll never beat yours. I can't wait until the berries come in this summer. I'll pick all you want." She got herself a glass of water.

44

When she turned back she intercepted a strange look between Hemma and Amy.

Not sure what was up with her friends, Marian held back her announcement until they were all at the table. Over a plate loaded with a pasty, gravy, steamed broccoli and corn-on-the-cob, she said, "I'm going to get my M.L.S."

Amy grinned in mid-chew. "Brava, girlfriend!"

Hemma paused with her fork halfway to her mouth. "Honey, that's *wonderful*. When did you decide?"

"Yesterday, when my period wouldn't start."

"Are you sure large life decisions should be made by hormones?" Amy licked butter off her fingers.

"I've had plenty of non-hormonal time to think it through." Marian frowned. "Now I'm not sure why I waited so long. I'd rather be done now than just beginning."

"You're a look-before-you-leap girl. It's exactly what you need to do." Hemma salted her corn. "It's important to take professional aspirations . . . seriously."

Amy excused herself for another beer.

"It's thanks to you, you know." Marian wanted to say more. She wanted to say there had never been anyone else in her life who had reached inside her and flipped on the poise, aspiration and determination the way that Hemma had.

"You'd have gotten there on your own."

"The pasties are incredible, thank you. What a treat."

Hemma sipped her water. Quietly, she said, "I treasure your friendship, Marian."

Amy slid back into her chair. "We both do."

Neither of them would meet her gaze. Marian didn't know what to think. She opened her mouth to ask, but the phone rang and Hemma hurried off to answer it.

She scraped broccoli remains into the composter while she worried that she had somehow made them nervous. Did they suspect how she felt about Hemma? Had they caught her spying on them?

They'd had seconds of the warm flan and moved to the living room when Marian couldn't stand it any longer. "Something's up. What is it?"

To her shock, Hemma's face crumpled in distress. Amy patted her partner's knee and said, "This is really hard. The hardest part."

"I don't understand." They knew. She'd given herself away somehow. She wanted to say how sorry she was, how embarrassed and sad, and how she never meant for them to know, and it wasn't Hemma's fault and Amy shouldn't be jealous. She had only realized they left their blinds open two years ago. It had been when she'd slept in the guest room for a while, after Robyn had left. It had seemed harmless. She watched out of love, not for kicks. She would never do it again. Her ears burned. She had to say it.

"Marian." Hemma's voice quavered. "I've been offered a tenured professorship in American studies at the University of Hawaii. And I'm . . . damn it . . ." She looked imploringly at Amy.

Amy, after squeezing Hemma's arm, said, "It makes too much sense. She's worked so hard. And for us it means we'll be retiring in better positions when the time comes. I'm in the process of securing a position as well. It won't cost me much in tenure. It's the chance of a lifetime for Hemma. You know how stiff the competition is . . ."

Marian could hear Amy's voice but her mind resounded with one word: *Hawaii*.

She realized Amy had stopped speaking. They were both looking at her apprehensively.

"You're moving." It was hard to breathe.

Hemma's lower lip quivered as enormous tears spilled down her cheeks. "It was such a hard decision to make. We don't want to leave here. Leave you and all our friends. The garden, the university . . ."

"When?"

"It's a terrible time to sell our house, but we meet with a realtor tomorrow. We didn't want you to come home from work and see a realtor's sign."

"It's certainly a wonderful opportunity." For a moment, Marian wasn't sure she'd spoken.

Hemma asked quietly, "Are you okay?"

Everything in her wanted to say of course she was okay. But that was a gigantic lie. She shook her head.

Hemma flew across the room to wrap Marian in her arms. "I'm so sorry, this is going to hurt us all. It was such a hard decision to make. Promise us right now that you will visit at Christmas. Bring us pickled ham."

Marian thought she laughed but she wasn't sure. Everything after that was a blur. Hemma looked wretched and even Amy wiped away tears. Hawaii. Why not Mars?

Thursday evening, June 5
No more Thursday dinners. No more voyeuristic participation in a life I'll never have. No more . . . no more anything. There aren't any words and I feel so empty.

Later that night she watched Amy hold Hemma against her as they stretched out in bed together, comforting each other with kisses and hugs. Hemma blew her nose as Marian's vision swam. Tears splashed on the windowsill.

When her vision cleared, Amy was kissing her way across Hemma's shoulders. Marian felt her stomach turn over and she backed out of her spare room. It was over.

All gone in an instant. The perfect beach, the perfect woman. A perfect picture of lovers hand-in-hand. Even the fantasy had been destroyed.

Part of her was happy for her friends. It was a big deal for Hemma. She knew they'd be fine. They were a wonderful couple. They'd make new friends, carve out a new life with the same care and patience with which they'd crafted their incredible garden.

Someone else would have pasties and gravy and berry pie, or whatever the equivalent was in Hawaii. Someone else would be lucky enough to be their friend.

47

Until that moment she had been numbed by her grief over losing Hemma in her daily life, even if they would never be lovers. But she was losing both of them, and the broad nurturing shelter of their relationship. They were her family, and along with Ellie, had been since she'd lost parents and brother that horrible year in Chicago.

She was abruptly aware that she could hear Hemma's voice. The rising croon she knew so well made her feel ill. She covered her ears, but the sound of their love rolled through her mind. It would never be hers.

She wanted to hate them and almost could. But then she felt so tired and empty she couldn't breathe.

She sank down in the hallway, sobbing. When Professor Hill padded up, she buried her face in the collie's fur and cried in pain. She was every bit the lonely, dried-up, frustrated, pathetic nobody Robyn had said she was.

4

Friday morning the hot spell eased. Liddy lounged in bed, reading and taking notes on the laptop she'd bought with the advance against expenses that writer Dana Moon had given her.

Robyn had said she was useless, but she was going to prove the bitch wrong. And prove her parents wrong, too, and several professors, as well as Miss Hoagie, her third-grade teacher, who had written, "Liddy's work would be excellent if she finished it."

She had an agreement with Dana Moon to provide no more than 400 pages about the inner workings of a teaching hospital and the obstacles a female doctor would face upon becoming its chief administrator. Liddy was starting with the more interesting tangent of women in medicine. Somewhere along the way she would get inside the hospital, preferably without becoming a patient.

Her mother hadn't wanted to believe in the job. "How can anyone want to pay so much for what will take you just a couple of months to do?"

"I think she understands that boiling down all that information to four hundred pages is where the real work is. Anyone can gather up facts." She had shrugged. "Professor Haughton recommended me."

The letter of recommendation was one of the high points of Liddy's varied and lengthy collegiate career. Though her ambitions as a student had wandered from English to public administration, sociology to physical education, she'd managed to impress more than one instructor across disciplines with her ability to quickly process vast quantities of information and regurgitate it in an organized, succinct fashion. She'd gone to college to learn, not to become.

Robyn Vaughn, one-time visiting lecturer at Cal in women's studies, had said she liked Liddy's bullet points. She'd said it again later that evening, with that cheap sexy laugh, while caressing Liddy's nipples. They'd been standing at the end of an aisle in the used bookstore when Robyn had surrounded Liddy with that perfume. How must she have looked for Robyn to have realized she could touch her that way within minutes of meeting outside class? The scent's effect on her had always been Pavlovian. She smelled it, she got wet.

"Fuck and fuck it, that's enough of that." Liddy set the laptop to one side before she gave into the temptation to hurl it against a wall. No more thinking about Robyn. She was done with that.

"A dojo, that's what you need. Find a class, a sparring partner. Though I pity my partner in this mood."

She was halfway through her shower when she realized she was talking to herself. Okay, she needed to get out.

The Golden Dragon Martial Arts Academy looked prosperous enough. Although the mats and equipment had a well-used look, none of them were threadbare, which was encouraging. The only people in martial arts who made real money at it were in the movies, but good instructors, in her experience, had no trouble keeping enough students to provide the basic necessities.

"I'm only here for the summer, and I'm worried I'll get out of shape," she concluded, after stating her current rank and past studies for the benefit of the man seated at the small desk.

It wasn't until the white-clad instructor stood up that she saw the red and black belt he wore. She had not expected to find someone of that rank in the middle of nowhere. What next, a bona fide red belt in Iowa fucking City? She'd yet to meet one in Berkeley.

Sensei Kerry looked her up and down. "Did you want to stay in shape or begin your progress from brown to black?"

"Stay in shape," Liddy admitted. "I'm not certain it's in the cards for me to be a black belt."

He smiled in the way of every sensei she had ever met, male or female. "It's not a matter of chance—"

"Chance is an excuse for lack of focus, I know." She clapped a hand over her mouth, then bowed out of habit. "I apologize, sensei."

He smiled and bowed slightly to accept her apology. "There is a class for purple and brown on Mondays, Wednesdays and Fridays at seven."

"Do you teach it?"

"There are also two assistants."

Remembering her manners, she asked meekly, "Would you do me the honor of allowing me to join your class?"

Again, the man disappeared into the mystery of a sensei. He seemed to be in his mid-thirties—only ten years her senior at most—but all senseis specialized in that remote air of a sage. "A brief test will be necessary."

"I have my gi, sensei, so at your convenience, I am ready." She felt a part of herself relax. This, at least, was familiar.

"Five minutes," he said, pointing to one of the square mats, then he left her to change and warm up.

She'd tried to work out after Robyn left, but Robyn had taken a few classes with her, leaving that musky smell impossibly in the changing room. She knew it was all in her head that she could still smell it, but she had not been able to shake it. It had been two months since she'd been to her classes. Another thing in her life she hadn't finished. Another thing that Robyn had managed to take away.

Well, at least she could stay in shape here. Her gi was a little more snug around the waist than it had been. Who would have thought Iowa City had a world-class anything besides drunken frat boys to offer?

Ignoring the few other students who were practicing with targets and pads, she ran through a few forms, then went to the mat the sensei had indicated, and knelt with her back to the center. Deep, calming breathing was easier than it had been in months.

Permission to spar came promptly and she squared off, aware that she was, indeed, being tested. It quickly became apparent that Sensei Kerry's belt was not a fake. His stance and blocking invited her to throw punches and level kicks at him that were well within her skills. As her strength and ingenuity waned, his mastery became more apparent. She was tested to her limit to parry his carefully conceived attacks.

She was pouring sweat after only a few minutes had elapsed. But she felt alive. She found herself grinning as she rolled off the floor from evading a kick and had the satisfaction of a returned smile from the sensei.

"You've had a good teacher," he acknowledged.

"You honor a humble student." She gasped for breath and added belatedly, "Sensei."

"I would enjoy learning from you," he replied, then dropped his guard to invite a series of jabs.

The feeling of intense focus was welcome. She loved karate and she was not going to let Robyn fucking Vaughn take it away. When the sensei invited another round of punches she twirled into an unexpected kick. She wasn't surprised when he blocked her, but she successfully evaded his counterpunch.

"Enough," he declared. They bowed respectfully to each other, and Liddy stripped off her sparring gloves. "Whatever it was that motivated you at the last, that is what you will need more of to move up to black belt. But I believe you can do it."

"I wish I was going to be here long enough, sensei." To her surprise she felt a small amount of regret that the end of July would arrive too soon when it came to the Golden Dragon.

"We will see what you can do while you are with us." He bowed again and became a businessman, proffering forms and requesting a credit card.

Back in the Hummer, Liddy grinned and turned up the radio. A tuneful song she didn't know explained that it took a little bit of this and a little bit of that. The sky was richly blue and Iowa fucking City wasn't so small after all.

She cruised into the Wal-Mart lot and shoehorned the Hummer into a parking space under the only trees. Sometime later she maneuvered her cart full of household essentials into what seemed to be the shortest line. As she reached for a tin of Altoids she recognized the voice of that stalker, Ellie. Swear to freakin' god, this town was tiny.

"You must be miserable, honey," she was saying. There was an indistinguishable reply. "They're your best friends. I don't know that many single girls who are so tight with a couple without, well, being *very* tight with the couple, if you know what I mean."

"I did *not* have that kind of relationship with them!"

Liddy wanted in the worst way to turn her head and figure out who Ellie was talking to. It was a rather interesting conversation. But she was afraid if she did, Ellie would see her.

"I don't think you did, of course. They define monogamy. Besides, you're practically virginal." Ellie made the other woman's chaste sex life sound like a bad thing.

"Don't, El. Not today. I don't think I can be jollied into a better mood."

The librarian, Liddy thought. Okay, Iowa City must be small if you trip over the town librarian everywhere you turn. She risked a peek; they were behind her and another line over. With luck, she would get out unseen.

"When Sandy and I split, you were the one who told me that life is change."

Marian's voice was low and harder to hear. "I'm sorry I was cruel. That couldn't have been comforting."

"It wasn't."

Liddy loaded her items onto the belt and dug in her shorts pocket for her billfold.

"I feel like I got hit by an anchor, Ellie. I just didn't see this coming." Marian sounded slightly choked and definitely sad.

Ellie's tone softened. "It wasn't comforting, but it was true. Sandy changed and so did I. Hemma and Amy are setting out to make some big changes. Our Friday evening meet isn't going to be the same."

"I don't change. Why does everyone else?"

Making small talk with the cashier left Liddy without the concentration necessary to continue eavesdropping. She forgot about the *Days of Our Dykes* conversation as she stopped to buy a cold soda, then rolled her cart toward her car. About halfway there she realized Marian and Ellie were off to her left. Marian gave Ellie a cheerless parting wave, then veered in Liddy's general direction.

Picking up her pace, Liddy reached the Hummer quickly and dropped her bags in the back. She heard Marian's bags rustle and realized Marian must belong to either the forest green Beetle to the right of her or the platinum Malibu to the left, all crowded into the meager shade. She didn't know if she wanted Marian to recognize her or not. Fate took a hand when Marian stopped at the Beetle and had no reason to notice Liddy on the far side of the Hummer.

Liddy had her door open when Marian snapped, "Damn it all!"

She stole a glance through the opposite window and saw Marian patting her pockets more and more frantically.

"Shit. Oh . . . shit. Ellie has them. For crying out loud, what else?" Marian dropped the two bags she was carrying. "Not that I

54

could even get in my fucking car with this gas-sucking monstrosity parked next to it!"

Then Marian kicked the Hummer's rear bumper.

Liddy was so surprised she just stood there, blinking. It wasn't as if Marian could hurt it. Marian kicked it again.

"Excuse me, but could you not do that—"

"Oh, hell!" They stared at each other, then Marian said, "I'm sorry. I can't get in my car."

Liddy saw that it was the truth. Damned Hummer. She'd been so jazzed from her workout that she hadn't realized she was inches from the Beetle. "I'm sorry, too. I did park too close."

"My friend has my keys. She's halfway home now."

"Can you call her on her cell? You could use mine if you need to." She wondered if Marian remembered their earlier meetings. Abruptly, it mattered that she did.

"She has a pathology about cell phones and brain tumors."

Liddy shrugged. "I'm sorry about your keys. Are you having a bad day?"

Marian nodded.

Liddy had only enough time to think, "This is what I get for talking to people, swear to freakin' god," before two enormous tears spilled down Marian's face.

It was incredibly awkward, standing next to someone who was silently sobbing. Excusing herself would be heartless. Yet what could she do?

After a minute she dug in her pocket for a tissue. "Here. And I'll take you to your friend's house for your keys. I'm not late for anything."

Marian covered her eyes with the tissue, and a small noise that belied the depth of her distress escaped her. It was the sound of a hurt dove.

Liddy felt empathetic tears start in her eyes. Hell, there was one thing she could do.

Marian didn't resist her head being pulled to Liddy's shoulder. Her arms circled Liddy's waist in complete surrender to human comfort.

"It'll be okay. Eventually," Liddy whispered. She wished she weren't quite so sticky from her workout. She had to add "eventually" because this was how she'd cried over Robyn. She'd cried and cried while Mom told her it would be okay, and then she'd cried because it pissed her off that her mother didn't understand that it would never be okay.

It was a few minutes before Marian stepped back abruptly, wiping her face. "I'm sorry—you must think me a fool."

"No, really. I've had to cry like that. I'll take you to your friend's for the keys."

Marian nodded and gathered her bags.

"You'll have to climb in through my door. I'm sorry I blocked you."

All Marian said, when Liddy activated the slide out step was, "How useful."

"It's that or dislocate a shoulder climbing in."

Very quietly, Marian replied, "Dislocating a shoulder is not something I want to repeat, thank you."

Liddy would have asked more about that, but Marian turned her face to the window.

After they were backed out of the parking space, Marian said, "She's in the Longfellow area."

"You'll have to point me the right way."

"I'm sorry. Head toward the university."

"That I can do. I have found even when I'm not looking for it, I always end up at the university."

"You could actually drop me at work. That's where I was going next. Ellie will drop off my keys if I leave her a message. I'm going to see her this evening, regardless."

Marian had presumed Liddy knew where her work was, so she obviously remembered her. Liddy felt oddly relieved. "Are you sure?"

Marian nodded. "I'm so sorry."

"Stop apologizing."

"It's a bad habit."

Liddy turned toward the river and then stole a glance at her passenger. "Did you want to stop somewhere to tidy up?"

"Do I need to? Shit, I'm sorry. Of course I do. I look like a circus clown after I cry."

"That's a little harsh," Liddy offered, though the comment was somewhat true. Marian's eyes were puffy and red, and she had telltale blotches of pink across her forehead and cheeks. She looked unhappy, deeply unhappy. "You could dash into the Java House. Coffee and a face wash."

Marian shrugged and Liddy had no idea what to make of that. "Half the people I know hang out there, though it is early for the Friday meet."

"Then where? Oh—look. I live a few blocks up on North Dodge, so it's no bother."

"I couldn't impose."

"Why not?"

Marian shrugged. "Thank you, then."

Liddy turned toward the house, then realized her offer meant she'd have to repark the Hummer in the driveway twice. She gritted her teeth as she waited for traffic to clear before risking the Scylla and Charybdis guarding the narrow entrance.

"Does it fit in the drive?"

"It would be easier without those posts."

"Why don't you park in the back?"

For a long minute, Liddy was torn between not wanting to appear incredibly stupid because she had no idea what the hell Marian was talking about, and a fervent desire to learn *exactly* what Marian meant. Practicality won. "There's a, uh, back parking space?"

"Didn't they tell you? A friend of mine dated the old owner, Marsha, who lives on Brookside now with her partner, Julie. Julie Y., not Julie S. Go up to the next street and turn left."

Liddy followed the instructions, then turned into the narrow alley that ran between the backyards of the houses. "I drove down here once, but there's no gate. Climbing the fence wasn't all that appealing, and I thought I might get towed."

"The realtor should have showed you. Marsha had a party and everyone came in the back way because Dodge is so busy."

Liddy pulled into the cleared area behind her house. "This is my parking space?"

"Sure. Usually there's room for two cars, but this one is, um, a bit large."

"Yeah, I know. It's a guilt gift from my biological father, heap big mountain macho man."

Marian nodded as if that made perfect sense to her. "The gate's buried under all that ivy. No wonder you didn't see it."

"Ah, the Hidden Gate. Sounds positively Jane Eyre."

Using bare hands, they stripped away a lot of the overgrowth. Sure enough, there was a lovely gate. Now she realized that if she'd been out in the backyard she'd have seen the stepping stones embedded in the too-tall grass. Sheesh.

"Thank you so much—I was thinking of selling the damned car."

"Everything works out for a reason." Marian's heavy sigh was at odds with her philosophical tone.

"Your friend has your keys so I can find out about this gate? The universe can be twisted."

"Tell me about it."

They tromped in the back door and Liddy remembered her manners. "Do you have time for some tea or coffee?"

"I don't, actually, but thank you." Marian headed unerringly in the direction of the bathroom. It was odd to think of her being familiar with a house Liddy didn't yet feel comfortable in.

Liddy put away her purchases while she waited. Marian returned quickly, her face a uniform well-scrubbed pink. Liddy offered her the bottle of Murine she'd fished out of her still unpacked toiletries bag. "It's bad for your eyes, but it's a special occasion."

Marian hesitated, then took the bottle. She carefully squeezed in the drops and wiped her cheek. "I'm sorry to be such a bother."

"It really is a bad habit."

Marian cocked her head slightly. "Oh, yeah. It is. I'm sorry, I'll . . . Forget it."

Relieved to see the glimmer of a smile, Liddy shepherded Marian back to the car. She realized then that the passenger-side steps didn't seem as helpful as the ones on the driver's side, and Marian had trouble reaching the overhead grab bar. She nearly helped, then thought she hardly knew Marian well enough for even a dispassionate hand on the backside.

They were halfway to the library when Marian broke the silence. "I'm not usually like this, just so you know. Rough day, that's all."

"Friends' moving can be traumatic."

Marian gave her a surprised look and Liddy flushed.

"Sorry, I overheard you in the store. I didn't mean to eavesdrop." The lie, she was sure, had tinted her ears red.

"I was worried you were a mind reader, that's all." Marian sighed. "It's hard not to have everyone know your business. It was a big adjustment when I first moved here."

"Where are you from originally?"

"Chicago. You?"

"San Bernardino, but I grew up in Berkeley."

Marian nodded as if she understood the vast difference, but somehow Liddy doubted it. "You'll get used to the close-knit community. You lose some privacy, but there are compensations."

"I'm only here for a research project. Until end of July."

"Oh. Weatherwise it's not the best time to see I.C."

"I can't imagine the dead of January being much better."

"No, you're right. April and September are lovely. The colors are beautiful."

Liddy pulled into the loading zone at the library. Marian gathered her bags and opened the door.

"I really appreciate this. If I can head off the posse I will."

Liddy laughed. "Okay, we'd be more than even. I'm not in the market. And I don't want to be in the market."

"Gotcha. Likewise." Marian arched an eyebrow. For the first time her hazel eyes held a smile. "The universe is twisted."

Liddy watched her walk toward the library entrance, wishing she'd had a moment to realize that if Marian wasn't interested in dating maybe they could, well, just be friendly. She had heard it was possible for two lesbians to hang out and not actually be dating.

Well, she reasoned, it was inevitable that she'd be in the library again soon. She abruptly realized that the prospect of another trip to the Iowa City Public Library wasn't the least bit unpleasant.

5

"Marian!"

Marian returned Jersey's wave and made her way past the growing line to drop off her backpack. Friday evenings at the Java House was a popular tradition for more than just dykes.

"Is it really true?" Jersey's electrician's belt was next to the lounge sofa, which meant she'd walked over from the freelance work she occasionally did in a couple of the restaurants. "The Rosings are moving to Hawaii?"

Marian nodded, trying to hide the surge of tears that welled up behind her dry, itching eyes. More salt, right, that would help. "Cool, you snagged the lounge area for us. It's easier on my butt than the chairs. Where's Terry?"

"She had an emergency at the clinic. A shepherd swallowed a Barbie head, apparently, and it hasn't made it out the other end."

"Poor pooch."

"That's so gross." Sandy settled into the easy chair next to Jersey and eased out of her loafers. "I have been on my feet all day. Last time I take someone else's classes on Fridays."

"It's the way all creatures work." Mary Jane, who had walked over from the library with Marian, dropped her satchel onto the chair across from Sandy. "What goes in must come out. Sit, Marian. I owe you from last week. Iced latte or mocha?"

"Swiss Chocolate Milk with a Costa Rican espresso shot. I'm going for the hard stuff."

"You'll be up all night," Sandy predicted. She worried a thread along the hem of her crisp T-shirt. Marian thought irrelevantly that Sandy never looked anything but cool and comfortable. She tried not to resent it.

"Caffeine, near as I can tell, doesn't keep me awake, but it sure makes me pee." Marian shrugged.

"Thanks for sharing, Marian." Mary Jane headed for the line.

Sandy dug a magazine out of her book bag. "Check this out, this month's *Cosmo*. A student left it. 'The Five Things That Turn Your Man Off.' I saw that and had to bring it. It's a scream."

Marian idly picked up the magazine, though heterosexual sex tips were as interesting to her as the science of pimples. Actually, since she had pimples, she was more interested in them. Maybe there was an article about hormones and skin eruptions.

"Heya, everybody!" Wen hooked the chair next to Marian. "Patty'll be here in a minute. She went over to Carrie's to get some more symphytum. Thank you, whoever got us these seats."

"Symphytum for your knee?" Marian couldn't remember what that herb was good for.

"Yeah, it's feeling lousy. I'm going to end up in a wheelchair, I think." With the nonchalance of long practice, Marian and Jersey helped Wen wedge pillows behind her back and under her knee. Severe arthritis had ended Wen's field hockey days in her early thirties, and had gradually restricted her mobility over the last five years. "Thanks, guys."

Sandy took Wen's proffered billfold. "The usual?"

"Have you heard about Hemma and Amy?" Jersey licked her stir stick.

"Yeah . . . two decaf Classic Whites. Thank you." Wen watched Sandy join Mary Jane at the end of the line before turning to Jersey. "No, what?"

"Hawaii," Jersey said. "Hemma got a tenured professorship."

"Holy cow." Wen stared at Jersey in disbelief. "She thought she'd never get it. The only people who care about American studies don't live in America. Hawaii? How great is that? I'll be lucky to get tenure in English lit in my lifetime, let alone at forty."

"Cool, huh?"

Marian thumbed through the magazine, unable to share in everyone else's delight at Hemma's good news. Some day she might be able to. But not today. Not this year. Possibly not this decade.

She wasn't the kind of person who told her friends every little thing in her life, but not being able to tell anyone about how unhappy she was made her realize she had never felt more alone in her life. How crappy was that? Surrounded by friends and none of them knew she was dying inside.

"Hard on you, though, huh?" Wen nudged Marian lightly. "When do they leave?"

"A month, I think." Marian swallowed hard and turned another page. Okay, she had to watch it with Wen, who could be as uncannily perceptive as Jersey was dense. "The house is going on the market."

"Oh, if Patty and I could afford it, I'd buy it in a second. That garden is incredible. Think of picking a salad for dinner every night, and those beefsteaks are amazing. But we just put all that money into the ramps and kitchen changes for me. And we'd have to build Patty a workshop, which would mean tearing up part of the garden, which rather defeats the whole purpose."

"I wish I could afford a house on my own," Sandy chimed in from the line. "Ellie and I share the house okay, but it's getting awkward. But neither of us can afford to buy the other out, even at I.C. prices."

63

"You should buy it, Marian. Sell yours and move next door."

For a forty-year-old plus, Jersey could be as practical as a teenager. Marian shook her head. "That would be nuts."

"Why?"

"I don't have the capital. My house is worth at least forty thousand less than theirs. I only own a house because of that once-in-a-lifetime insurance settlement from my folks."

Jersey's usually clear expression clouded. "Oh. But it'll be hard to have other people work in the garden, won't it? After you helped build that arbor? And the fountain wall?"

"Tell me about it," Marian muttered.

"Sorry."

"No, I'm sorry, Jersey." Marian managed to look up. "I'm depressed about it, that's all. I am happy for them, really."

"Understandable." Wen prodded the magazine. "What *are* you reading?"

"The five things that turn a man off, if you can believe that."

"As if," Sandy snorted. She set two coffees in front of Wen and returned her billfold.

"Oh, what are they?" Mary Jane set a frothy cup in front of Marian before settling with a sigh of relief into the chair next to her. "I want to know if I'm ever with one."

"I want to know, too," Jersey chimed in. "Maybe I did them and that's why I'm with women now."

Marian ran a finger up the side of her cup and popped the resulting dollop of whipped cream into her mouth. Inner Therapist, who always showed up when she was depressed, pointed out that she was using coffee as a narcotic. So arrest me, Marian thought waspishly. She summoned a cheerful expression with difficulty. "Number one: saying 'you're better than all the other guys I've been with.'" She had to grin at the howls of laughter that erupted around her.

"I think that would be the wrong thing to say to any lover!" Wen rolled her eyes.

"Oh, I don't know." Mary Jane adopted a philosophical attitude. "Sometimes that's exactly what I want to hear."

"Oh, really, that can be great to hear. I'll vouch for that." Sandy gave Jersey an arch look.

Jersey blushed furiously. "Honey!"

Marian glanced at the others, trying not to laugh.

"Oh, shit," Jersey muttered. "I just said 'honey' to my ex! Thank goodness Terry's not here."

"It's okay." Wen reached across the table to pat Jersey's hand. "As long as you stick with 'honey' for everybody you'll never get it wrong when it really matters."

"Honey or baby." Mary Jane had that too-innocent expression again. Marian thought she could only pull it off because she was in work drag. In her days-off jeans and men's tank tops, Mary Jane looked far more earthy.

"Just how many partners have you had?" Sandy fixed her brown eyes on Mary Jane. "You never admit to anything."

"First, tell me how many is too many."

"A thousand."

"I've been with fewer than that. So far." Mary Jane's blue eyes were definitely twinkling as she nonchalantly examined her nails.

Marian had to sigh. From all appearances, Mary Jane was single. Why couldn't she be in love with her? Why did it have to be Hemma? She blinked furiously. "Item two is too much talking during sex."

There was a thoughtful silence.

"Not during," Sandy finally said. "I can see that."

"Well, depends on the topic during. Not about the grocery list—that would probably dim my pilot light." Wen craned her neck to glance at the door. "No sign of Patty, huh?"

"If it's an hour we'll send a rescue team over to the herb shop." Jersey gave Wen a meaningful look.

Wen shrugged. "I hardly think that will be necessary. But if she doesn't get here soon I'm going to drink her coffee, too."

Marian finished a deeply satisfying slug from her drink. "Item three is sort of on the same topic. Talking too explicitly."

"Poppycock." Mary Jane gave Marian her best managerial stare. "That's absurd. A well-chosen sweaty word or two at the right moment can be a wonderful thing. Whatever are their reasons?"

"They say that most guys like the idea of a having a wild time with a wild woman, but in actuality they still prefer to believe the women they're with are less experienced than they are. Too much hot talk can bruise their ego."

"That's bizarre." Sandy was shaking her head. "Okay, it's not like I was with a lot of guys before I figured out I was gay, but they would have all agreed with Mary Jane on the purpose of some hot talk. Their egos are not that fragile—there's Patty."

"What's the scoop?" Patty lowered herself to the cushion near Wen's feet and reached gratefully for the mug Wen indicated. Marian admired Patty's biceps, not for the first time. She even found a little grin when Patty caught her at it and winked. Patty had always been good for her ego. "By the way, Carrie will be along in a half-hour, she thought."

Marian recapped the list so far, and each viewpoint expressed. "Your turn, Patty. What's your opinion of hot talk during sex?"

"I like it. I like knowing what she wants. I think all talk is important. I mean, if she's talking about her grocery list while I'm making love to her, that's a message."

"Good point," Jersey conceded.

Wen squeezed Patty's leg with a sad smile. "Yeah, it probably means I need a pain pill."

Patty colored slightly. "Honey, anything you want, any way you want it, you know that."

"I know, it's just . . ." Wen's eyes filled with tears.

Mary Jane leaned over to put one hand on Wen's arm. "Hey, it's okay."

Wen managed a watery smile. "I'm sorry, everybody. I had a doctor's visit this morning."

The sigh of understanding that Marian let out was shared by everyone. Wen was always bruised emotionally and physically after seeing the doctor. She patted Wen's knee. "If I had magic pixie dust I'd use it all on you."

"Thanks." Wen's shrug was obviously forced. "Another topic please—I appreciate the diversion."

Sandy dabbed at a dribble of cream that had smeared the sleeve of her trim pocket T. "I have a general question on the topic of hot talk. After all, I'm reentering the dating pool. Or trying to. What kinds of things work as hot talk and what don't?"

Mary Jane ended the expectant silence with, "Don't everybody look at me."

"You had a definite opinion about it, that's all." Sandy pointed the stir stick at Mary Jane. "Spill it."

"It's too contextual to say categorically what works and what doesn't." Mary Jane rolled one shoulder expressively. "A woman can say 'roll me over' in the right tone of voice and I'll break out in a sweat."

I ought to be in love with Mary Jane, Marian thought while she chuckled. No doubt the sex would be grand.

Ellie appeared in the doorway and navigated the bottleneck around the line. "Sorry I'm late. Here's your keys. Lucky you got a lift." She hooked her hair behind her ear. "Any sign of her? Is there mocha frozen yogurt?"

"Thanks, no, and I think so." Marian slipped the keys into the pocket of her shorts. She realized she didn't want to admit who had been her benefactor. "We're discussing what works as hot talk in bed."

"I've always liked *more*. It's a hot word, said the right way." Ellie glanced momentarily at Sandy, then headed for the line.

"Mary Jane also said tone of voice can be more important than the words." Wen added huskily, "Roll me over, baby."

Mary Jane fanned herself with a napkin. "Don't do that here, honey, it'll get you in trouble."

Marian blinked as she processed the look that passed between Wen and Mary Jane. Abruptly, it seemed to have far more levels than normal. Wen and Patty had been together ten years, at least. Maybe there had been a thing between Wen and Mary Jane before that. Inner Historian made a note about another possible entry for the Iowa City dance card.

Jersey abruptly perked up. "There's my girl."

Terry had to say several excuse me's to get past the line, and she reached their cluster looking mildly annoyed. "Hey all, the dog's gonna live, but it wasn't fun."

"Glad you made it," Jersey said after Terry kissed her.

"Tell me I can have a double shot," Ellie pleaded from the line. "I worked on a knee and a tennis elbow this morning. Then I went on ripping out Jenny's guest bathroom pipes. Got that mostly done. My daddy'd be proud."

"I know I'm going to have a double shot," Terry said. "I don't know how you do it, juggling two careers."

Ellie shrugged. "Physical therapy I love, but plumbing pays the bills. I broke another nail, though." She turned to give her order.

"Item four, then," Marian pronounced. "Don't look in his eyes for too long."

"I don't like eye contact," Jersey said. "I don't know why. It's not just that it's really intimate."

"It interferes with the fantasies running in my head." Sandy glanced briefly at Ellie in line. "I feel things more if I close my eyes."

Marian looked up from the magazine. "What if what you're looking at is really arousing?" The image of Hemma's naked back flashed in her mind and she fought back a flush.

"I'm with Sandy," Patty said. "Blindfolds aren't so much kinky as they are permission to focus on inner feelings."

Marian saw a flicker of sadness cross Wen's face, then it eased into a smile edged with wickedness. "I wish it didn't say 'sleep' in neon orange, though."

Patty swatted her partner's hand. "Enough of that. What's the last one?"

"Oh." With difficulty Marian dismissed the image of buffed Patty in a blindfold, and scanned the remainder of the article. "Don't cry."

"Sometimes, crying is the whole effing point of effing." Sandy studied her napkin. "Catharsis is catharsis. I've gone to bed with people just to have a great cry afterward."

"It can pay to have tissues near the bed," Terry added.

"Since when?" Jersey shifted in her chair so she could lean against Terry next to her. Terry shrugged and kissed the top of Jersey's head.

"Crying doesn't put me off, as long as she's crying for the right reasons," Mary Jane said quietly.

"It's my orgasm and I'll cry if I want to," Marian pronounced. "Given my hormones, any excuse is good enough."

"I thought you weren't seeing anybody." Sandy drained the last of her drink and frowned at the empty cup. "The ginseng peppermint tea is hard to beat. I may have to have another."

Marian couldn't resist. "Orgasms do not require another person in the room." She didn't even blush, though she thought of all the times she had watched Hemma, then gone to bed to fantasize about her.

"I know that. I'm single, too, remember?" Sandy studiously did not look up as Ellie joined them.

"I don't know what you all are talking about, but there's only one thing on my mind." Ellie slouched into the chair next to Marian. "And that's the mystery woman. I can't get anywhere, and it'll make me crazy to watch someone else bag her."

"Oh." Patty straightened in her chair and slowly brought her focus to Marian. "That reminds me—doesn't she drive that enormous yellow Hummer? And wasn't that you, Marian, getting out of that monster this afternoon?"

The blush started somewhere in the small of her back, and traveled rapidly over her shoulders, up her neck, then turned Marian's ears so red she felt the heat on her scalp. She hated it when everyone stared at her.

"Ellie had my keys," she finally muttered.

"Well, well, well." Head to one side, Mary Jane appraised her with surprise. "I didn't know you had it in you."

"I didn't do anything."

"Then why are you red as a tomato?" Ellie bounced in indignation.

Marian wanted to crawl under the table. "Because I kicked her car."

They all blinked at her. Terry finally spoke. "You kicked her car? You. Kicked her car."

"Ellie had my keys, and I couldn't get in my car even if I wanted to because this behemoth was two inches from my door. I was having a bad day, and Libby gave me a lift to work, that's all."

"Libby?" Ellie's eyebrows were so far down they were nearly touching. "Her name is Libby?"

Marian nodded. "I read it off her license."

"And her car was there next to yours by accident and you didn't mention this to me?"

"I didn't know it was her car when I kicked it. I figured it was some damned Californian with more money than sense."

Sandy spread her hands. "Maybe it is. Who knows anything about her?"

"California plates?" Ellie's tone was dangerously quiet.

"Yes. She's here until end of next month, El. Doing research of some kind. And not wanting to date. Not in the market."

"For a lift to work, you covered a lot of ground."

I'm not going to tell about the trip to her house, Marian thought stubbornly. They can't make me.

"That's her," Jersey said in a loud whisper.

All heads but Marian's turned toward the door.

Ellie stood up for a better look. "Who are those two she's with?"

"Students," Patty said. "Headache bait."

"Hey," Jersey protested. "I'm a student when I'm not stringing wire, remember, and I do not give anybody, including Terry, headaches."

"You're not the typical student," Patty reminded her.

Ellie plumped back into her seat. "This is gonna kill me. Two students talking to a woman of that quality."

Sandy abruptly pushed away from the table. "I want to go see who the band is tonight."

There was a pointed silence after Sandy left.

"I can't go on pussyfooting around like I'm not trying to date." Ellie's chin was at its most mulish. "She knows I've been dating."

"You don't have to wave it in her face, do you?" Marian had never been really close to Sandy, but she'd always felt Sandy was kind and generous. In a lot of ways, Sandy and Ellie had been an odd couple. Ellie was as mercurial as Sandy was placid. The breakup had been Ellie's idea.

"What if I told you we broke up because she was having an affair?"

Terry's coffee slipped out of her hand and she steadied it on the table. "Did she say that?"

"You're kidding!" Wen paused with her coffee halfway to her mouth. "I don't believe it."

"No way," Marian protested. "Why keep it to yourself until now?"

Ellie stabbed her frozen yogurt with the spoon. "She never said that. I just said what if I told you—and you didn't believe me. I really think you all like her more than me."

Marian tried to soothe Ellie's mood. "It's not a matter of choosing sides, but Sandy has—"

"I have to go," Ellie snapped. "I'm bad company right now. Hope the band is good." Napkins fluttered to the floor in the wake of her rapid departure.

"She'll feel better tomorrow," Marian muttered.

"Incoming," Wen whispered.

"Huh?" About then Marian realized Libby had left the counter and was making a beeline for her. She had something in her hand.

"Hi," Marian said, knowing she was bright red. "Thanks again for the lift."

"You're welcome. It was no bother, really. But I think this fell out of one of your bags. Not my brand. I, um, didn't have anything to put it in. Sorry."

Marian took the tampon box with all the nonchalance she could manage. "Mine. Sorry I left it." She quickly stuffed it into her backpack.

"I had a feeling I'd run into you here."

"It's a habit." Marian didn't recognize the pathetically squeaky voice that was coming out of her throat. Feeling very awkward, she said, "Everybody, this is Libby."

"Liddy. Sorry, it's Liddy."

Mary Jane laughed outright. "Marian is usually clear on her facts."

"I didn't get a good look at it," Marian muttered. She had not thought it was possible to blush harder than she already was, but she'd been wrong.

Liddy shrugged, but Marian thought she looked annoyed. "It happens a lot. Nobody wants to believe I was named after some reactionary nutcase my biological father idealized. When G. Gordon had his radio show I wanted to just change it to Libby, believe me."

"It must be a trial," Wen observed.

"Only around the politically correct, and we have lots of those in Berkeley. One righteous woman told me I ought to change it to something woman-identified, as if I'd chosen it, and continuing to use it was an affront to ovaries everywhere."

Jersey grunted in agreement. "I'm Jersey, and I was told recently that my name glorified mobsters."

"Ignorance isn't anyone's exclusive property, is it?" Mary Jane peered into her nearly empty cup. "That went down way too easily."

Marian sensed it was that moment when she ought to ask Libby—Liddy, you fool!—to join them. But the last time she'd done that it had been Robyn. But if any of the other women did it, Liddy became *her* casual coffee date type person, not Marian's.

Oh, bother. Desperately, she tried to sound businesslike. "We got a new text on medical ethics you might be interested in."

She felt the combined gazes of all of her friends on her face.

Liddy's smile wasn't quite relaxed. "Thank you, that's very helpful. I'll look for it—same call number?"

"Yes. It should be there tomorrow."

"Great. Well, thanks." Liddy nodded and went back to the counter for her latte. The two students she'd been talking to had already left. Without looking in Marian's direction she slipped out the door again.

After a long silence and a great deal of ice-chewing, Mary Jane observed, "Really, Marian, I didn't know you had it in you."

6

Liddy was out the door of the Java House before she realized she wished someone had asked her to join them. Marian, maybe. Yes, that would have been nice. Marian was strange, but interesting. It bothered her that Marian had gotten her name wrong, but it had happened before. Robyn had gotten it right, so it was no indicator of personality.

She toyed with the idea of going back inside on some pretext. The area where they were all seated was all the way on the other side of the counters. She could have pretended to study the art exhibit, or to be contemplating the wildly colorful selection of travel mugs, but that would have only looked casual if she hadn't already scurried out the door.

It was definitely cooler than it had been. Liddy guessed eighty, but with the humidity it was hard to gauge. With a sigh she turned in the direction of the live music she'd heard from the far end of the

Pedestrian Mall. It was a pleasing mix of bluegrass and pop. She skirted people playing chess with pieces the size of ten-year-olds and dodged the lemonade vendor moving his cart. It was crowded and she supposed she would be lucky to find a place to sit.

As she approached the nexus of the play structure, fountain and hotel entrance, she saw that she'd supposed rightly. Parents already occupied curbs, benches and retaining walls that faced the enormous jungle gym. The fountain had been turned off to make room for the band. Folding chairs had been set up in a crescent around the band, but all were taken by music lovers.

The music was good, though. She could manage for a while, standing. Feeling homesick, she bought a falafel and ate it while leaning against a column outside the hotel.

She watched clusters of people meet, mingle, disperse and regroup. If her gaydar was working, ten to fifteen percent of the crowd—including the parents—was lesbian and it was, well, comforting. It all looked so *normal*.

Curious about how women paired off—Berkeley was her only data sample so far—she took note of the number of obviously butch/femme couples. At first she thought there weren't that many. Everyone was dressed the same, in shorts and tank tops or T-shirts. It was too warm for anything else.

Okay, next to the slide was a definite butch. The shorts were men's, the T was black and her hair was buzzed to a quarter-inch flattop.

It became an interesting exercise after that. Subtle cues she hadn't really considered before were more obvious to her. Tops with scalloped hems and hair accessories might indicate a femme, while a baggy tank top over a sport bra and long, plain shorts could denote a butch. Then a trim woman in square-legged men's running shorts and a tank top graced with a bow and spaghetti straps came into view. Mixed signals, Liddy thought. That or she just wears what feels comfortable. And why not?

She caught a glimpse of herself in the hotel windows. She supposed the ponytail was the biggest hint that she had femme tendencies. That, nail polish and the strappy sandals she'd chosen over her usual Tevas. She sometimes took umbrage at the femme label, however. It depended on who used it and what was meant by it.

Something slammed into the side of her knee. She looked down in time to see a toddler taking a very deep breath. When the breath came out, the screech nearly drowned out the band. Liddy looked around frantically for parents. People were looking. They probably thought she was killing the kid.

"Whoa, buddy!" A short-haired brunette scooped up the howling child. "Sorry. He doesn't look before he runs."

Relieved, Liddy said, "It's okay." She rubbed her knee for a moment, but it wasn't even bruised.

Another brunette with equally short hair rushed up. "Is he okay?"

"Yeah, honey, he's got a hard head."

The newcomer shot a look at Liddy that suggested her knees ought to have air bags. She took the boy away from her partner. They looked too much alike not to be a couple, Liddy thought wryly. "I'll get the boo-boo bunny."

"Don't worry about it," the first woman said to Liddy in parting. "He's got a head like a rock." She grinned. "That's from her side of the family."

Liddy grinned back. Wow. Mom-type dykes weren't exactly known for their sense of humor in Berkeley. She took care to turn herself more toward the play structure. With luck, she could avoid injuring more children with her inconveniently placed knees.

An all-too-familiar voice behind Liddy startled her. "Come here often?"

Fuck and fuck. "No, I don't."

Ellie at least was looking at her eyes this time. "I apologize if I've been obnoxious."

"I hadn't realized," Liddy said wryly.

"I've been told I come on a little strong."

Liddy shrugged. "I'm not in the dating pool."

"So Marian tells me. She's a sweet person, my best friend is."

"She seems so."

"I can't figure out why she's still single."

Great, now Ellie was matchmaking. Liddy drained the last of her iced coffee. "Some people are meant to be single. The whole world doesn't need to couple up."

"I think you're right in general, but not about Marian. She's a born nester. But she had a relationship with a woman who turned out to be a vicious nutso and she's a little gun-shy now, too."

How many ways do I have to say that I'm not looking, Liddy thought. She was sorry about the nutso, though. Marian really was a bit odd, but she was quietly, gently butch in a way Liddy had always found appealing. "You don't have to explain about nutso exes. Been there, done that. Everybody gets gun-shy about settling down."

"Yeah. I'm not sure I'm meant to be settled down." Ellie tossed her hair over her shoulder in a gesture she had to know was attractive and flirtatious. Ellie would tip anyone's meter to the femme side of the scale, and Liddy doubted Ellie would mind anyone's saying so. "But I do like to have fun."

Hell. Was there no getting rid of this woman? "I'm here because I'm getting over a bad breakup. And I don't do the rebound thing. That's gone sour on me too. In fact, my luck with women has been so bad I'm thinking of going back to men."

"Oh, what a waste." For a moment something other than lust gleamed in Ellie's eyes. "I seem to make the mistake of repeating bad relationships."

"Tell me about it."

Ellie's gaze followed the chaos of children circling the play structure. "We could have a drink and I could tell you some long, sad stories."

For a moment, it was an appealing prospect. The Pedestrian Mall was so alive with music and motion that being alone was doubly poignant. She said bluntly, "I wouldn't want to lead you on."

Ellie laughed. "I got your message. Besides, Marian and I never compete."

Liddy couldn't help but ask, "She doesn't want to date me, does she?"

Ellie colored slightly. "I'm sorry, that was not the right thing for me to say. Marian doesn't date. At least not so you'd notice." She frowned. "She really is a sweet, kind, considerate person. She's smart, funny, holds up her end of the conversation. I'd marry her myself if she wasn't my best friend. Not that she'd have me."

"I thought partners were supposed to be best friends."

Ellie stepped out of the way of a massive side-by-side stroller. "I've never believed that one. I mean, how many partners do we have before we're through? And how many best friends? Seems to me the best friends are the rarer commodity. I'm not going to fuck that up by fucking her, you know?"

Having thought Ellie was a bubble-headed stalker, Liddy was surprised by the cogency of the statement. "I do see what you mean."

"Everything I fuck I fuck up." Ellie glanced away for a moment. "Well, I'm glad we got to talk. I *was* obnoxious, wasn't I?"

Liddy grinned. "Yeah. Just a tip for the future. Make sure the new woman doesn't actually hear you call her Fresh Meat."

"Oh." Ellie swallowed. "I'm so sorry. You weren't meant to hear that. It's a running joke."

"I understand. Definitely not politically correct."

"Heavens, no. We have plenty of that here, but not when it comes to dating. Though no one wants to support my position, which is if we really want to break the patriarchy, we'd all be single and sleep around."

Liddy laughed outright. "Spoken like someone in favor of redistribution."

"You got that right—Hemma Rosling, it's really you! Hey, girl, congratulations!"

Liddy watched Ellie throw her arms around a slender, dark-haired woman who had to be of Middle Eastern descent. Another woman, with pale skin and lively green eyes Liddy found slightly mesmerizing, watched indulgently.

Hemma returned Ellie's hearty hug. "Thanks, El. I'm still stunned. Going back and forth between giddy and sad. Amy is coping better than I am." She separated from Ellie and took the green-eyed woman's hand.

"You're doing fine, honey." Amy patted Hemma's arm.

"I'm so pleased for you. What an opportunity." Ellie stepped back to include Liddy in the conversation. "Hemma just got a tenured professorship in Hawaii."

"Congratulations," Liddy said politely.

Hemma held out one hand. "We haven't met."

"Liddy Peel." She shook hands with Hemma and then Amy, both of whom repeated their names with a firm grip. How very coupled, Liddy thought, to have the same last name.

"Liddy?" Ellie cocked her head to one side. "Marian had it wrong. How amusing."

Liddy shrugged. She realized she was getting a bit old to have a love-hate relationship with her name, but there it was. She was certain Ellie wouldn't care for being introduced as Effie.

"What brings you to Iowa City, Liddy?" Amy regarded her intently.

She found herself explaining about the research job and giving every detail she knew, which wasn't much, about the eccentric Dana Moon. The conversation lasted until the band packed up, and Liddy was surprised to realize it was nearly dark. She had thought the days would be endless in Iowa City.

"What's the occasion?" She gestured at the departing band.

"Occasion?" Amy gave her a puzzled look.

"For the live music."

"Every Friday night during the summer," Amy said. "It's usually very good, too. The Ped Mall's the place."

"The occasion is that the students are gone," Hemma added with a smile.

Liddy winced. "Ouch, I was a student until a month ago."

"Sorry." Hemma was still smiling. "Now you're a grownup."

"Ouch again. I'm not sure I want to be."

"That'll pass." Hemma touched Liddy's arm briefly then turned to Ellie. "Was Marian at the Java House?"

"Yeah. Speaking of devastation."

Liddy watched Hemma's eyes fill with tears. Amy's green eyes glittered as well.

Hemma shrugged helplessly. "I know. We're so close. I almost turned it down, but what kind of professional would I be to turn down the chance of a lifetime because I love my next-door neighbor to pieces?"

Liddy felt a couple of dots connect in the back of her head. The conversation she'd overheard at Wal-Mart, Marian's tears . . . Hemma and Amy were the reason why. They both certainly seemed like nice women, the kind of professors she would have liked to have had more of in her college career.

"Human," Ellie said. "You'd be human. But I understand. And certainly Marian does."

"Maybe she'll get out more," Hemma offered. "I've often thought if not for us sucking up her social time she'd find someone to make her happy. She deserves it."

"I was just telling Liddy that," Ellie volunteered.

Now three pairs of eyes turned to her speculatively. Goaded, Liddy said firmly, "I'm not in the market."

Hemma sighed.

"Amy! Say it isn't so!" A group of women who seemed to know Amy from the university descended on them, and they had all heard the news.

Liddy was politely trying to follow the conversation when out of the corner of her eye she saw the unusual motion of someone backing away. She focused over Hemma's shoulder to see Marian turning to walk quickly away from the gathering.

"I really do have to get going," Liddy said to Ellie, who was engrossed in an increasingly flirtatious conversation with a woman who taught composition.

Ellie nodded pleasantly without breaking her conversation. Liddy said a general, "Nice to meet you all," and then hurried in the direction Marian had gone.

She didn't know why she was following Marian. Their contact had been, well, unusual. She just remembered that sound of suppressed pain from this morning.

When she saw Marian's figure ahead of her she slowed, still unsure what motivated her. And now that she had pursued Marian, how would she get her attention?

When Marian turned to wave at a passing taxi, Liddy set aside feeling foolish and said just loud enough to be heard, "Need another lift?"

Marian wheeled around. Liddy saw the glitter of tears across her cheeks and something inside her melted.

"I can't make a habit of this," Marian croaked. She cleared her throat. "I forgot to ask anybody for a ride to my car."

"And you didn't want to cry in front of Amy and Hemma," Liddy prompted softly.

"Damn, you're way too observant." Marian scrubbed her cheeks with one hand. "Good thing you're not sticking around."

"My car's on the street. Linn? At least I think that was it."

They walked in silence until Marian said, "Thanks for my tampons. I actually need them."

"Well, otherwise why buy them? Oh, damn it all!" Liddy had to jump twice to snatch the parking ticket off her windshield. "Second one!"

"You could park on the ramp," Marian suggested.

"So I've been told, but what the heck is 'the ramp'? I didn't see a store like that on the map. There aren't any signs."

"The ramp," Marian repeated. "Parking ramps. There are several."

"Do you mean a parking garage? I saw the sign for one, but it's attached to the hotel. I figured it'd cost an arm and a leg."

Marian shrugged. "I doubt by California standards it does. A couple of dollars for an evening."

"Oh."

"Otherwise, you can expect a lot of those." She pointed at the ticket. "I.C. is notorious for the number of parking tickets it gives out. College town."

"Okay." Hell, who would have thought Iowa fucking City was so secretive about places to park, Liddy thought. "I didn't think I needed a local guide to Iowa City, but obviously I do. You should put your services on eBay."

"If you were a student you would have received the standard orientation." Marian shrugged again.

Liddy watched as Marian tossed her backpack up into the car, then hauled herself into the passenger seat. For a moment she thought she might have to lend a hand, which made her look again at various parts of Marian where a push would help.

Marian was shapely, for a librarian. Hell, she was shapely for any profession.

Flustered, she forgot to trigger the steps on her side and had to haul herself up with less than her usual aplomb.

"Show-off," Marian said.

They stared at each other by the dim illumination of the dashboard lights. Damn, Liddy thought. I am not lusting after Marian the Librarian, swear to freakin' god. Why would I? I hardly know her. Why am I trembling?

"The idiot behind me has me blocked," she muttered.

Marian glanced back and said, "Those big SUVs. How rude."

Liddy snorted, put the Hummer in drive, and went smoothly over the curb in front of her. "I like these kinds of parking places."

Was that a giggle? Had Marian the Librarian just *giggled*? Her eyes were dark and glittering. Liddy realized she'd give a million bucks—and the Hummer—to know what went on inside Marian the Librarian's head.

≈∞≈

Marian fought back another uncharacteristic chortle. She was almost hysterical. She'd been crying all day, and it suddenly didn't help that Liddy Peel seemed to have the ability to make her laugh.

"Do you know the way to Wal-Mart?" She hoped her car was still okay.

"Honey," Liddy drawled, "I'm a Wal-Mart femme."

"Femme?" Marian looked Liddy up and down. "The car sort of counteracts the femme energy."

"No reason a femme can't have butch toys."

"Okay, I agree with that." Marian kept her tone light. "Ellie is the highest femme I know, and yet she looks good in work overalls and a plumber's tool belt. Some women actually find a femme in butch trappings very sexy."

Liddy opened and closed her mouth, then finally said, "I could pull a logging truck with this baby."

"Why?"

"What a good question. I don't know how to do it, either."

Reassured that Liddy wasn't into random acts of machismo, Marian asked, "What's a Wal-Mart femme?"

"A whole lot less expensive to live with than a Saks Fifth Avenue femme."

Hell, she was going to laugh again, and if she laughed she'd start to cry. "Makes sense to me. But if we're going to Wal-Mart you should have turned at that light."

"Hell." Liddy braked and swung into the middle turning lane. "Sorry about this, but I'm from California."

Marian had just enough time to grab the arm rest before Liddy whipped into a U-turn. Liddy certainly knew how to drive, terrifying though it was.

"Oh, fuck me! Fuck—is that a cop?"

Marian glanced. "All I see is the bar of lights on top of the car, but, okay, now that they're lit up, yes, I'd say that was a police car."

Liddy pulled over to the curb and fumbled in her front shorts pocket for her wallet.

Trying to be helpful, Marian asked, "Can I get the registration out of the glove box?"

"Sure," Liddy muttered. She rolled down the window.

Marian could hear only half the conversation, but Liddy was peppering each sentence with enough "sir" and "yes, officer" to please a drill sergeant. Liddy took the registration Marian held out, then opened the driver's door.

The officer stepped up on the running board to shine a flashlight inside. Liddy flipped a switch and the interior lights came on.

After a moment, Marian said, "Oh, hey, Johnny."

"Friend of yours?" Johnny Trelow's stern expression softened slightly.

"Yeah. She's from California. I should have warned her about U-turns. The law's different here I'm sure."

Johnny stepped down to the pavement again and said sternly, "If you'll promise me you'll make her go to motor vehicles for a basic book—"

"I'll make sure she does," Marian said solemnly. The noise Liddy let out was a blend of irritation and relief.

"Next time," he added, "go around the block if you have to."

"Yes, officer," Liddy said meekly.

As his boots crunched back to the car behind them, Liddy closed the door. "What just happened?"

"Johnny and I were in the last year of the history program together. I eventually became a librarian and he became a cop."

"History degree? Ah, now that's useful. I've got one of those myself."

"There ya go. Smart career move."

"Tell me about it." Liddy's sigh was heavy.

"That's why I'm getting a second master's in library and information science."

"That's why I'm doing other people's research for them. Why is he still there?"

"Waiting for you to pull out into traffic again. For your safety."

"Hell. Okay. If I can stop shaking."

"Johnny's not a redneck."

"I'm from Berkeley. All cops are bad, in theory."

Liddy carefully pulled out into traffic and only spoke after the patrol car passed them. Marian gave Johnny a cheery wave, which he acknowledged with two fingers to his brow.

"I owe you big-time," Liddy said.

"It's okay. He might not have written you a ticket anyway, given the out-of-state plates and that you weren't being a jerk."

"My biological father may not have been around to teach me much, but he did impress upon me that being rude to a cop would only get you remembered in court."

"And he got you this car."

"Vehicle, please," Liddy scolded.

The laugh escaped before Marian could shut it down.

"That's better," Liddy said. "Laughter is good for you."

Marian choked back the sob that followed. Her throat was very tight as she said, "So I've heard."

Liddy turned into the Wal-Mart lot and coasted to a stop behind the Beetle, now very lonely under the trees.

"I think your car would fit in the cargo area of this one."

Another laugh bubbled out and Marian dropped her head into her hands, choking between tears and hysteria.

"You're not okay, are you?"

She shook her head. "But I will be."

"That's the important part."

Marian struggled for a semblance of control. This was absurd, crying in front of a stranger. Something about Liddy made her feel safe enough to cry. "Have you ever had a balloon pop right in your face?"

"Yeah." Liddy's tone indicated she didn't understand the purpose of the question.

"Dreams can be like that."

After a long silence, Liddy said quietly, "I don't look forward to that happening to me, but I suppose it happens to everyone, eventually."

"I didn't see this one coming."

"They seem so nice."

Alarmed that Liddy would figure out her secret, Marian tried desperately to pull herself together. "Great cooks. I'll miss the free meals."

"Right."

"Thanks again." She found her backpack on the floor and opened the door. "How do these steps work?"

"Allow me, madam." To Marian's surprise, Liddy leapt out her door and hurried around the car. "You didn't have to get out."

Liddy pressed a button for the steps and held up one hand like a footman. "Your Beetle awaits, milady."

"This is serious role reversal," Marian muttered. She didn't like being made to feel short, and the distance from the seat of the Hummer to the ground was intimidating. Besides, there was nothing a mildly shy, modestly butch and proudly independent woman objected to more than being helped out of a car.

Not a car, she reminded herself, a VEE-hickle.

Liddy held her hand for a moment longer than necessary. "Are you sure you're going to be okay?"

"Yeah. I'll be fine." Liddy still had her hand.

They stood there for a minute. Marian began to think of ways to pull her hand free that wouldn't be rude, then realized she didn't necessarily want to hurry. Liddy made her laugh. And her hand felt exceedingly warm, in a most pleasant way.

Finally, Liddy said shakily, "I'm not in the market."

"Neither am I," Marian answered.

When it was clear Liddy was going to kiss her, Marian felt as if another person had taken over. Inner Slut reminded her it had been *years* since she'd really been touched, and Inner Prude even admitted there was nothing wrong with a kiss between two unattached people.

The first touch of Liddy's lips sent what rationality she had left reeling. Sweet and firm, Liddy's lips woke up nerves in the back of Marian's legs she hadn't felt since Robyn. No, she thought, get Robyn out of your head and kiss this woman properly. Kiss her . . .

Sweet lord, she smelled good. Very different from Hemma . . . No, no, don't think about Hemma, kiss *this* woman, the one in your arms.

She didn't remember exactly when she dropped the backpack and threw her arms around Liddy. She felt Liddy gasp, and their mouths opened to each other.

Liddy's tongue was direct and inviting, then playful. Marian kissed her in return, feeling woefully out of practice, but she felt a shiver run through Liddy before Liddy pulled away.

"I swear," Liddy said, "I did not mean to do that."

"Sorry?"

Liddy's arms went around her waist. Marian surrendered to a hungrier kiss, Liddy's tongue teasing and dancing, leaving little doubt as to how agile it might be other places. She abruptly realized she was deeply aroused, the reality of which shocked her so much she pulled her head back. "I'm not like this, really."

"Neither am I."

The third kiss was as electric as the first two. Marian felt as if she'd never realized her mouth could be so alive, so aware. She'd been kissed before, but Liddy's kisses seemed different. Very different.

"Unbelievable," Liddy murmured against her mouth.

"What?"

"I didn't think—this isn't what . . ."

"Me neither."

"I'm not and you're not, and we're not . . ."

"No, we're not." Marian gently pushed Liddy away. "But thank you. You're good for my ego."

"Yeah. I mean, you're good for mine."

"You must get lots of offers." Marian immediately wished she hadn't said that. It sounded like she was fishing for Liddy's dating history.

"Don't flatter me."

"It's a simple statement of fact. You probably get hit on a lot." What Marian really wanted to ask was why Liddy was kissing *her*.

Liddy took a deep breath. "Okay, I'll admit that's true. But not by women with half a brain, usually."

Marian felt a deep rush of pleasure. She'd much rather be thought smart than cute. Then she remembered she was supposed to be heartbroken. Where had all the tears gone?

She touched Liddy's chin with her fingertips. "Thank you."

"Anytime." Liddy's grin was endearingly crooked.

"See you around." Marian was proud of herself that it wasn't a question.

"I'll be coming to get that book you mentioned," Liddy said as Marian unlocked her door. "Around one? Before I get some lunch?"

Marian held back what surely would have been a silly schoolgirl simper and said instead, "One is always a good time for lunch."

She was certain that Liddy was watching her drive across the parking lot. When she reached the street she tooted the Beetle's horn and heard an answering bellow from the Hummer.

She laughed again, and noticed the moon had risen.

Friday evening, June 6

I'd have gone to bed with her. Not HER. Her. Liddy Peel. Except I'm bleeding like a stuck pig—what a gross expression. I never feel this way on Day 1. But I did and I do.

What's wrong with me? This morning I was too depressed to write and now I feel like I'm sailing on moonlight. Over a virtual stranger.

This is how it happened with Robyn and I'm not making that mistake again.

Crap on a biscuit. Did I stay in love with HER because she had no risk? How stupid is that?

Great. Now I'm angry. What's wrong with me?

❧

"I swear, Trombone, if you puke in my shoes again I'm giving you to a violin factory!"

The Russian Blue gave Marian a withering look worthy of an empress before stalking out.

Marian scraped the bottom of her favorite clog, then rinsed it under the kitchen tap. Perhaps she should put her shoes up on something. Sometimes Trombone was worse than a toddler.

Professor Hill whuffled at her heels, then sniffed up the back of her legs. "What? Oh, smell something new?" Marian flushed. "That's Liddy. I don't think you'll, well, maybe. I don't know."

She poured out food for both animals and grabbed some crackers for herself. Dinner had been too long ago.

Still muttering, she went up the stairs. Hill padded along behind her, his tail creating a breeze around Marian's knees. Abruptly, she noticed the accumulated pet hair in the corners of each tread. Tomorrow morning, she thought, it was time to do some cleaning.

She wearily stripped off her shirt and bra. Tomorrow morning, she recalled, she had volunteered for the early shift at the I-CARE breakfast. It sucked that it was her weekend to work. Cleaning would have to wait until Monday, her next day off. What a shame.

The mirror was disappointingly the same. Her cheeks were still chipmunkish, her eyes still unremarkable, her lips still too thin.

Those lips had kissed a virtual stranger tonight. Goosepimples blossomed all along her arms as she realized that a virtual stranger—an attractive, intelligent, witty stranger—had kissed her first. Had kissed her more than once.

Neither of them was trying to have an affair, but still, being found worthy of such world-class kisses had felt truly magical. She didn't have Ellie's looks or personality, or Amy's height and competence, not even Patty's muscles or Wen's intuition. She didn't have an herb shop and a kind soul, either. But Liddy had still kissed her. It didn't make sense.

It had felt wonderful.

It was habit more than anything else that took her to the doorway of the spare room. After Robyn had destroyed her life she'd slept in this room to avoid Robyn's scent and the memories of her body. Even when she finally went back to her own room, she still checked on Hemma and Amy every night.

It had at first seemed like looking in on a secret world, one too fantastic to ever include her. Shocked by the violence of Robyn's departure, she'd been comforted by the vision of a life that seemed to go happily and smoothly. Watching Amy and Hemma make love had felt like a panacea for her own emotional hurts.

She curled up in the rocking chair and closed her eyes. Falling in love with Hemma hadn't stopped her from dating, not at first. Once she accepted that Hemma would never look at her the way she looked at Amy, Marian had hoped someone else would eventually supplant Hemma. Even so, when Robyn Vaughn had used those oh-so-perfect moves to get Marian into bed on their first date, Marian had known Robyn would never be Hemma in her heart. She'd thought they could make a go of it, though. She'd hardly expected Robyn to be what Robyn was.

The sound of Hemma's voice made her open her eyes again, and she gazed at their window. Tears welling in her eyes washed prisms of light over the sight of Amy's long arms around Hemma. It had seemed so perfect, their life. Maybe it was. But living through their lives had kept her from living her own. Duh, she thought. Like Dr. Phil wouldn't have figured that out in two seconds.

She was so tired and so hurt. She'd been thinking about Robyn too much, and after two years, she'd hoped Robyn would be forever out of her head. She could feel the box of Robyn Ruins almost speaking to her now, reminding her she'd never dealt with it. She'd had enough therapy before leaving Chicago to know that she would open the box "when the time was right." Well, it's not the right time, she thought bitterly.

Hemma's laugh flowed across the night and Marian dashed away the seeping tears. Rising, she pulled the window down to meet the sill and wearily made her way back to her own room, her own bed. Hill planted himself on the other side of the mattress and sighed happily. Moments later Trombone took up her place in the precise center of the bed.

This is all okay, Marian thought. My life is okay. I have a job I love, friends who care for me. I care about them, too. It's enough. Hemma wasn't going to be a big part of her life from now on, she acknowledged sadly, and she'd just have to survive.

She was too depressed to cry. An hour ago she'd been lit up by moonlight, she reminded herself.

Oh, joy.

Mood swings, the worst equipment on the playground.

7

The lunch date with Marian wasn't until one, Liddy reminded herself. It wasn't even a date. Not even a plan, really. It wasn't as if she'd actually asked Marian to join her for lunch.

The idea of possibly having lunch left her feeling unsettled. She tried to read and continue taking notes, but every few minutes she got up to pace.

Ridiculous, she told herself. If you can't work, just get out of the house.

She had not had a chance to browse at Prairie Lights, she recalled. Having a roomy parking space behind the house instead of shoehorning the Hummer into the driveway made it easy to just pop over to the Ped Mall. So it was only ten a.m. She'd treat herself to a new book to read just for pleasure.

She parked gleefully on the ramp, which looked remarkably like every parking garage she'd ever seen, and joined the steady stream of people meandering through the hotel and out into the bright Saturday morning sunshine near the fountain and play structure.

The mall was more crowded than she'd expected. There was no sign of Marian near the library, not that Liddy really looked for more than three or four minutes. She would just walk the couple of blocks to the bookstore as planned. At the first cross street she made a quick detour to the Java House. Not that she expected Marian to be there either.

Tropical iced tea in hand, she was nearly to the bookstore when she saw that the far end of the pedestrians-only area had been set up with picnic tables and awnings. Something smelled tasty.

It was a pancake breakfast. How Midwestern, Liddy thought. How All-American and Family Values.

She would have turned away, superior and amused, if Marian hadn't been sitting at the closest table, eating pancakes and sausages while chatting with a man Liddy didn't know and a woman who had been with Marian at the coffeehouse last night.

Her feet didn't even hesitate. The next thing she knew she was standing in Marian's line of sight.

Marian stopped chewing for a moment, then swallowed. "Oh. Hi."

Be cool, Liddy told herself. Sure. "Is Iowa City one endless round of amusements and parties?" She gestured at the balloon dangling from the awning support pole.

"We try not to let the rest of the world know." Marian indicated her plate. "They're not quite done serving and the flapjacks aren't half bad if you want to support the cause."

"Marian will save you a seat," the other woman said neutrally. Remembering her insights into butch and femme attire of last night had Liddy analyzing the woman's sleek linen trousers and unembellished button-down shirt. The strong, silent type, Liddy guessed.

"Sure," Liddy managed. Why was she so preoccupied with putting the dykes in this town into categories? "I'll be right back."

She expected the Boy Scouts or the Lions Club or even the Shriners with their tasseled hats, but instead she found herself tithing to the Iowa Center for AIDS Resources and Education in honor of Pride month. Swear to freakin' god, Liddy thought. Where else but in Iowa would anyone raise money to fight AIDS with a pancake breakfast?

She turned down the sausage and helped herself to butter and strawberry jam. Hoping her high color was mistaken for a response to the climbing temperature, she settled next to Marian and tried to think of something clever to say. Lacking that, she blurted out, "Why a pancake breakfast?"

The man said, "Why not? I'm Eric, by the way."

"Forgive my rotten manners." Marian swallowed and cleared her throat. "Liddy Peel, this is my colleague, Eric Waters. We hang out as often as possible at the reference desk. And this is my boss twice-removed, Mary Jane Heyer."

"I always feel so important when Marian refers to me as her colleague," Eric said dryly.

Marian gave him a fond look. "*Associate* sounds illicit to me and *coworker* doesn't convey my vast respect for your skills."

Eric seized Marian's hand. "Will you marry me, dear woman? I can't get any of the straight ones to."

Liddy laughed. "Is there a policy about fraternizing?"

Mary Jane looked stern when she answered, "I'd have to frown upon this particular match."

"Dang it all." Eric forked up the rest of the pancakes. "So much for someone to hem my shirts and cook my meals."

"And now," Marian said to Liddy, "you see why Eric is still single."

"This may be the wrong place to meet straight women," Liddy suggested. "Especially of the doormat variety."

"I know, I know." Eric sighed heavily. "This looks like a pancake breakfast, but it's really the beginning of the Dyke Social Season. I'm just an accessory for my beloved colleagues, who are so single they have to take a straight man to the I-CARE breakfast."

Mary Jane threw her balled napkin at him. "I can have you shelving books all day, you know."

The plump blonde Liddy had nearly knocked over—was it only two nights ago, Liddy wondered—stopped at the table and put her hand on Marian's shoulder. "Thanks again for doing the early shift and then some, dear. Moving all those sausages is not fun. I wasn't kidding when I said half the volunteers don't show, was I?"

"Carrie, only for you would I pack that many sausages."

Mary Jane's guffaw turned heads. "I didn't know you were that kind of girl, Marian!"

Liddy watched Marian's cheeks stain with red. But her eyes flashed with humor as she replied, "Who needs to be, with you around?"

Regaining what seemed to be habitual composure, Mary Jane simply said, "Touché, my dear Miss Pardoo."

Carrie gave Mary Jane an indulgent look. "You can be *such* a juvenile sometimes."

"Gotta stay young somehow," Mary Jane quipped.

"And I'm surprised at you, Marian, stooping to her level." A light breeze rose for a moment, and Liddy caught the muted, refreshing scent of rosemary and oranges.

"With Marian it's the other way around. Everybody has to stoop to her level," Eric said quickly.

Marian gave him a cross look. "That's right. From the double entendres to the short jokes. What would I do without my friends?"

Liddy realized Carrie was holding out her hand. "I'm Carrie Bloom. We haven't been formally introduced."

"Liddy Peel." She added awkwardly, "I'm here for the summer doing research."

"A pleasure," Carrie said.

Liddy murmured something likewise. That lovely aroma of oranges and herbs was coming from Carrie. Her dun-colored clamdiggers and loosely crocheted top attractively framed a gener-ous figure that only a fool would dismiss as maternal. Liddy wasn't sure but she thought she spied the outline of a nipple ring. Carrie was very sensuous in a flowery granola Birkenstock way. Okay, she thought, considering that you didn't come here to date, you're notic-ing every single dyke in this town.

"A dab of essential lavender oil will take the sting out of that mosquito bite," Carrie volunteered. She pointed at Liddy's shoulder.

"Really?" Liddy peered at the bite. It didn't itch yet. "I'll keep that in mind."

"I carry it at my shop, or you can also pick it up at Soap Opera. It all comes from my garden no matter where you get it. Oh—time to break down the serving area. Thanks for your support, everybody."

Liddy struggled to remember something Ellie had said earlier in the week. "Is she the one with the holistic love couch?"

Eric choked on his water and Mary Jane's eyebrows rocketed upward.

After she stopped coughing into her napkin, Marian said, "I guess you could say that. The grapevine in this town never ceases to amaze me."

Mary Jane added gently, "Carrie looks at sex as a spiritual bond-ing, not an emotional one." She struggled to appear serious, but the smile that twisted the corners of her mouth was winning. "I would venture to say if you're invited to share the sacrament with her, you won't regret it. But the invitation isn't a guarantee."

Marian was bright red again. "You'll be asked right away or not at all. And whatever magic Carrie's conjuring, I have to admit it works for her."

"Not just for her. Not given that you're red as a pomegranate."

"Oh, thank you for pointing that out, Mary Jane." Marian took a deep breath, but stayed quite red. Liddy rather liked it. "I was simply trying to say that Carrie may be the most content person I know. She has exactly the life she wants."

"Or she's learned how not to want what she doesn't have," Liddy observed. "I have problems with that one."

If anything, Marian grew redder. What did I say, Liddy wondered.

"I'm afraid it's time for me to go to back to work," Mary Jane said.

"Me too," Eric added. "Lucky Marian with the morning off."

Marian retorted, "I was up at five, how lucky was that? And I work until closing tonight."

Eric looked at Liddy and fluttered his eyelashes, the picture of innocence. "How lucky *you* are remains to be seen, doesn't it?"

"Jesus," Marian muttered. "Do you guys give each other points for making me blush, or what?"

Eric nodded serenely as he rose. "Mary Jane's ahead right now."

"It's like shooting fish in a barrel," Mary Jane said. "Which is not to say it isn't fun."

They wandered off, laughing, and Liddy watched Marian's face slowly resume a more normal hue.

Marian sipped her water. "Who needs friends . . ."

"When do you have to be at work?"

"Two."

"Oh, so you *would* need lunch around one."

"Sure."

"And if you needed lunch at one—" Liddy glanced at her watch—"two hours and fifteen minutes from now, where would a person find you, needing your lunch?"

"Hell, the way this week has gone, you'd find me at the Java House face down in the Colossal Chocolate Cake."

"That bad?"

Marian's gaze lifted from her empty paper plate and Liddy found herself falling into a mix of golds and greens. *Hazel* was just too ordinary to describe Marian's eyes. Her breath stopped for a moment.

"My week is definitely getting better," Marian murmured just before her lips touched Liddy's in a sweet, lingering kiss.

Swear to freakin' god, Liddy thought. If anyone had told her she'd get kissed at a pancake breakfast in Iowa City, she'd have never believed them. Marian tasted deliciously of strawberry. Then the kiss wasn't sweet anymore, it was wet and hot, and needles of electricity shot up and down the insides of Liddy's thighs.

Where, she wondered, had Marian the Librarian from Iowa City learned to kiss like this? Light touches were followed by brushes of lips and a fleeting touch of her tongue that left Liddy feeling as if she'd never considered the passion a woman's mouth could hold before. Which was ridiculous. She'd been kissed plenty of times.

But not like this.

It felt so good that it took her a moment to realize that Marian had pulled away. She was belatedly aware that she had a stupidly satisfied grin on her face and she attempted to conjure up some dignity.

Marian wasn't blushing. If anything she looked smug.

"I could go away now and look for you at the Java House at one," Liddy finally said.

Marian's fingertips touched the inside of Liddy's forearm. "If that's what you want."

"Or we could have lunch now." Her arm tingled where Marian was lightly brushing it.

"We just had breakfast."

"We could skip the food and make it a really long lunch."

Marian's gold-green eyes were serious. "I'm not ready for more than . . . this. I'm hardly prepared for how this feels." Her fingertips traced the inside of Liddy's wrist.

"I wasn't suggesting we go somewhere and . . . you know." Part of her had been. And she was the one who hated being presumed available. Damn, now *she* was blushing. "Maybe we could go to a movie. Or see the sights. Or something. Since we're both here and I assume you've got the time to take pity on a California girl who doesn't know her way around."

"You know your way around fine. Just watch those U-turns." Marian's eyes were sparkling now. "But okay, maybe I can give you a tour of the lovely lakes and point out native flora and fauna."

98

It was the last thing Liddy usually wanted to do, but right then she'd have gone anywhere Marian suggested, on the hope that sooner or later Marian would kiss her again. Swear to freakin' god, Liddy, what happened to pledging off women and sex for a while? Marian the Librarian is what had happened, she told herself. "You're on."

Marian carried their breakfast detritus to the nearest trash can. Liddy watched her walking back, so enamored of the way the olive T-shirt clung to Marian's curves that she didn't read the lettering at first. When she did she burst out laughing.

"What?" Marian abruptly looked nervous.

"Are you?" Liddy stared pointedly at Marian's T-shirt.

Marian glanced down, then the tips of her ears tinted pink. But her voice was nearly a purr when she asked, "Which part?"

"I already know you're a librarian. Can I really check you out?"

"This is a public place." Marian slid back onto the bench next to Liddy. "And there are children about. So I don't think checking me out is a good idea."

Liddy leaned forward until her lips were a half-inch from Marian's. She waited until Marian half-exhaled in anticipation, then slowly, firmly pressed her lips to Marian's. Marian gasped again as Liddy nibbled on Marian's lower lip, then kissed lightly across Marian's mouth. "Tell me then."

"Tell you what?"

"The last bit on your shirt. If I checked you out, would I find you Dewey?"

Marian's smile reached her eyes, making them shine. "Those wacky librarians do like a pun."

Liddy snickered, then whispered in Marian's ear, "But are you? Dewey?"

"I'm not joking about that." Marian leaned back and all the laughter was gone. "And I'm a bit surprised by it and more than a little scared. I'm not like this, usually. The one time I was . . . impetuous . . . ended very badly."

Liddy's thoughts—against all her better judgment—of pleasant noontime dalliance fizzled out. "I can understand that. Besides, neither of us is in the market, remember?"

"Oh, I remember," Marian said. She rose and gestured for Liddy to precede her out of the roped-off area. "I think our brains are not listening to our bodies, though."

"More like the other way around."

"Marian, hold up!" They both turned to watch Ellie scurrying toward them.

"Hey, Ellie. You've met Liddy, right?"

"Yeah, we talked last night—hey, was Sandy here this morning? Have you seen her?"

"She left maybe a half-hour ago, why?"

"Her mom called. Her dad's had another small stroke and she'd like Sandy to drive over to the hospital if she can. It didn't sound urgent, but I think Sandy'd want to know right away, but she's not answering her cell."

"Where have you looked?"

"I thought she'd be here, so this is my first stop."

Marian dug in one of the many pockets of her cargo shorts, came up with a cell phone and dialed a number. A moment later, Liddy offered hers to Ellie.

"I hate these things," Ellie said, but she took it gingerly, pressed on, and started punching buttons.

Marian's poised, modulated voice made Liddy feel a bit dizzy. Marian the Librarian from River City could do phone sex with a voice like that. "Hey, Terry, Sandy wouldn't by any chance be bringing Buster in, would she? No, just trying to get her a message. Her dad's at the hospital again. Thanks."

Ellie was far more agitated. "Hey, Patty, was Sandy going to play tennis with you later? I really need to get ahold of her."

In five minutes, Liddy thought, every dyke in Iowa City would be on the lookout for Sandy.

Marian abruptly waved in victory. "She is? I should have thought of you first. Yeah, just tell her to call her mom, but it's not serious. Thanks, Mary Jane."

"Oh, of course." Ellie handed back Liddy's phone. "Thanks, I appreciated using it."

Marian said, "It's one place she'd switch her phone off. I should have called there first."

"Okay, that's a relief." Ellie's usually perky expression was dimmed. "I hope her dad's okay. I like her folks. They're sweet. Maybe I'll get flowers and go over later. He hasn't been well at all."

"I bet Sandy's mom would like something other than hospital food later on," Marian suggested.

Ellie brightened. "Sandwiches from Hy-Vee. Thanks, M'Sue."

"M'Sue?" Liddy watched Ellie hurry in the direction of the library.

"Marian Sue. Marian Sue Pardoo, if you want the whole deal. I can't tell you how pleased my entire third grade was that it rhymed."

"Ah."

"And?" Marian turned away from the library. "My car's this way."

"And what? We could take my car if we're going exploring in the countryside."

"I told you my middle name in a scary fit of self-revelation. I wasn't planning on leaving any paved roads."

"But we could in the Hummer, you know. It's got a winch."

"So what's yours? I don't think we're going to need a winch. Besides I need to move my car to the ramp near work."

"Okay, we'll take your car."

They walked in silence for a minute, then Marian said, "Is it a secret, your middle name?"

"Emma."

"A lovely name, what's wrong with it?"

"Nothing. Just . . . say my whole name."

"Liddy Emma Peel. It's very—oh."

Liddy waited for Marian to tease her, but all Marian did was chuckle quietly. She explained quietly, "My legal last name is Hartwell. But my mom remarried right after I was born and I've always used my stepdad's last name. So the Emma Peel thing wasn't even on purpose."

"That sort of makes it worse, doesn't it?"

"Yeah. It wasn't too bad until cable brought back the Avenger reruns. I was so teased in school, especially when I took up karate."

"I always loved Diana Rigg. I wanted her to read to me. And kick my brother across the room."

"Hey!" Liddy stared at the pavement. "What are these?"

Marian paused. "Nice, huh? You're looking at the Iowa Avenue Literary Walk."

Liddy carefully stepped over the words engraved in a binocular-shaped bronze plaque sunk into the pavement. "'I have noticed before that there is a category of acquaintanceship that is not friend-ship or business or romance, but speculation, fascination.' Jane Smiley. Interesting."

"All the quotes are from people with ties to Iowa. I'll show you my favorite, right up here."

It felt odd to be walking along while staring at the sidewalk. Liddy stopped to read another quote, set off by gold letters on a manhole cover. "'We are what we pretend to be, so we must be care-ful about what we pretend to be.' Kurt Vonnegut. Yes, that makes a lot of sense."

"This is it," Marian said, pointing.

This plaque was book-shaped. "Mildred Augustine Wirt Benson—that's a mouthful for a name. 'I'm afraid there's more to this than appears on the surface.'" Liddy frowned. As a favorite quote it seemed obvious.

Marian's smile broadened. "There's more to her name than appears on the surface. You might know her better as Carolyn Keene."

"Oh!" Liddy grinned. "Nancy Drew."

Marian nodded enthusiastically. "That's her. She was the first woman to get a journalism master's here at U of I."

"Cool."

"Speaking of names, I am curious about your name, though. Your father chose it?"

Liddy sighed as she fell into step with Marian again. "It contributed to the divorce. Mom was out of it—nearly died—after I was born. I'm glad she didn't. Anyway, my father filled out the birth certificate and Emma, a family name on my mom's side, became my middle name. Liddy hadn't even been discussed, but my father thought G. Gordon was a freedom fighter. He has a 'Nixon was Framed' T-shirt."

"You don't see much of him?"

"Not much. We get on. It's okay. But if we didn't have blood in common we'd have nothing in common, you know? My brother is turning into him, though."

The Beetle chirped at their approach. What a cute little car. Small, compact but loaded with personality. It suited Marian. Liddy oozed down into the passenger seat. "Wow. The view is different from down here."

Marian grinned as she turned the key. "See that handle over your door?" The engine purred loudly as she reversed out of the parking space.

Liddy looked up. "Yeah."

"Just remember it's there."

Liddy didn't really appreciate what Marian meant until Marian gunned the engine to make it through a yellow light at a left turn. The low car swooped through the intersection while Liddy fumbled for the grip and leaned into the turn for all she was worth. "You don't drive like you're from Iowa."

"Neither do you," Marian commented.

"You're going faster than the speed limit."

"Uh huh."

"I thought it was a rule here that everyone drive one mile an hour below the speed limit."

"I'm sure it is. But I learned to drive in Chicago. Six Polish uncles taught me how. My mother's maiden name was Myslakowski."

"That explains it. Six teachers, all men." Liddy held her breath as Marian gunned her way onto the freeway, cutting smoothly over to the fast lane.

"That looked closer than it was," Marian assured her. "I love my baby. She's got great maneuverability."

"Where are we going?" The large mega-mall loomed, but they didn't exit in that direction. Liddy looked back at it with longing.

"I'm not sure yet," Marian answered. "But we'll use the interstate to get there."

"Why?"

"I take joy in getting on the freeway and leaving at the very next exit. It drives nearly everyone I know here batty."

"That is how we do it in California."

"In Illinois, too. But not in Iowa. In Iowa—hold on." Marian whipped around a semi, then scooted into the slow lane where she proceded to pass the cars in the fast lane. "In Iowa, the interstate is for going from one state to another. If you're getting on the interstate you need a map, a cooler with drinks, and an extra gas can just in case you get caught in the vast distances between towns."

"There are some vast stretches," Liddy said. "I drove them."

"Coralville Lake, that'll do it."

The Beetle purred down the off-ramp for North Liberty. Liddy wondered if there was there a Central Liberty, or a South Liberty. In minutes subdivisions and farmhouses gave way to shoulder-high fields of corn and tall thickets of berries. Marian pressed the on button and soothing Bach flowed out of the speakers, at odds, Liddy thought, with the zooming pace of the little car.

"Over there! Deer!" Marian pointed. By the time Liddy looked they were out of sight.

Without thinking, she said, "Do you make love the way you drive?"

Marian's jaw dropped. She stared at Liddy for a moment, then back at the road.

"I'm sorry, I didn't mean to be—"

"No, I guess it's a fair question. I was thinking about the answer. I don't think so."

She slowed the car, although Liddy couldn't see why. There was no one else on the road with them and Marian was now at a crawl. "You're starting to frighten me."

"Don't mean to." She stomped on the gas and they shot forward again, regaining their earlier breakneck pace. "Yes, I think I do make love like I drive. Depends on the passenger."

Liddy had to laugh, but a little voice inside was whispering, "Manic depressive."

Really, she thought, what did she know about this woman? Okay, she has friends, and they seem to like her. She's a fabulous kisser. She cries at the drop of a hat. She's tenderhearted to be so sad that friends are moving away. She's still hurting about the nutso ex. She's a fabulous kisser. Her boss likes her. A straight guy wants to marry her. She drives like a fiend.

She was a *fabulous* kisser.

Robyn had been a fabulous kisser too. Nearly as good as Marian. And everyone else had seemed to think Robyn was a-okay until she went bonker kitties.

She realized that Marian had slowed again, but this time to a moderate pace. "I'm sorry, I needed to blow out the cobwebs. I really didn't mean to scare you."

"I wasn't scared. Just thinking."

"About?"

"Cornfields."

"Hard not to. The lake we're going to is just the other side of this mountain."

Liddy rolled her eyes. "Mountain?"

"Get with the program. You're in Iowa and that's a mountain."

Thinking of the Rockies she'd crossed on the way to Iowa, Liddy said, "If you say so."

"What were you really thinking about?"

"That I don't know much about you." Liddy admitted the truth without really meaning to.

"Thought so."

They turned onto a side road with only the measured strains of Bach to break the silence. At least Liddy thought it was Bach. It was one of those pieces that made Liddy think of sewing machines but somehow, with Marian, it didn't seem so deadly dull. Marian downshifted and Liddy had to admit there was a bit of a grade. "Mountain" was still a stretch, though.

As they crested the hill, Marian said, "The only thing I do violently is scrub my floors. I figure the floors don't care, and I'm actually healthier for it."

"I save my violence for the dojo."

"And brick walls."

Liddy cocked her head and then remembered her attack on the building at the Ped Mall. "Oh. That wasn't . . . I don't usually do that."

Marian let out a noise of pure chagrin. "I don't usually have mood swings so severe I need an oxygen mask. So we're even."

They coasted to a stop at an overlook. Not expecting much, Liddy got out of the car and followed Marian to the shade of the only tree. "Oh!"

"It is nice, isn't it?"

Their elevation was only a few hundred feet above the surrounding area, but the rolling fields and thick oaks lining numerous waterways were more obvious than Liddy had yet seen. The countryside was gently alive.

"I think of Iowa as very female." Marian gestured at the panorama. "I suppose most rural agricultural areas are, but it's also the roundness of the hills. Instead of a plotted out checkerboard, the rivers and creeks create curves in the roads and fencing. It's really a beautiful day for June. The haze can be bad in the late summer."

"It's lovely. Womanly, yes. Like a Wyeth painting."

"Yes, I've always thought so." Marian pointed at different fields, naming the likely crops. "Not that it's all that hard to guess what it is. Corn, oats, soybeans and Huskie fans, that's what we grow in Iowa."

Liddy chuckled and followed Marian back toward the car.

"Do you feel like a walk? There's a nature trail along here, and we can get some wonderful views of the lake."

"A walk would be great. Work up an appetite for that lunch."

Marian threw a grin over her shoulder and led Liddy onto a leaf-dusted trail. For the first few minutes Liddy just admired the view, and it wasn't nature she was looking at. Marian's hinder was wonderfully framed by her khaki shorts, and the lean legs were tanned and shapely. Marian's soft butch physique was put together in a very attractive way.

As they continued to climb, Liddy strained not to pant as she kept up with Marian's rapid pace. She was awfully glad she was wearing her Tevas. Marian pointed out a deer hideaway, gopher holes, a poisonous weed and trees with antler scrapings. Okay, Liddy thought. Marian was one of those outdoorsy gals. Marian knew all the stuff her biological father always wanted Liddy to absorb about the great outdoors.

She weighed the pros and cons. Know the names of gopher diseases versus fabulous kissing. Well, the kissing was so far winning, but she hoped there was no test administered at the end of the walk.

" . . . heard a word I've said."

"I'm listening," Liddy protested. "Just, well, not a lot."

"I'm babbling, I know. I'm nervous."

"Not really. Why?"

Marian stopped abruptly and Liddy realized how quiet it was on the shady path. There was only the distant drone of an engine to break the stillness. "Why am I nervous, you mean?"

"Yeah."

Marian ran one fingertip down Liddy's bare arm. Liddy couldn't stifle her responsive gasp. "Because of that."

Liddy swallowed hard. "Okay, I'll admit that makes me a little nervous, too. I'm not this way—"

"Me neither. As we keep telling each other. And the last time I felt this sweaty this fast with someone I got hurt. Badly."

"Me, too. So how come I'm not scared?" Had she been the one to step forward or had Marian? Had they both? Could Marian tell how hard she was breathing and that it had nothing to do with the hike? She wasn't in Iowa City looking for love, for sex, for anything except to get away from the anger and the hurt Robyn had left in her life. That and a paycheck.

Marian seemed to miss nothing. "I *am* scared. I think this would count as rebound for me." Her short laugh was strained. "For a lot of reasons. And that's not fair to you."

"Even if the paint peeled?"

"It's never that easy. Great sex does not a good relationship make."

"But neither of us is looking for a relationship." Liddy wondered exactly what she was trying to argue Marian into. She didn't want to let anyone close right now. But her body was acting like a teenager's.

"Sex without the prospect of a U-Haul?" This time Marian's smile was warmer. "I don't think lesbians do that."

"We could pretend we're guys." Swear to freakin' god, Liddy, did you really say something that stupid?

"You are not a guy." Marian leaned slightly closer. "Unless you are wearing the most incredible prosthetics money can buy."

Damned boobs. Damned nipples. She could hardly blame their obvious prominence on its being cold. "They're real," she said wryly. "Pure female under here. I have to say, you also seem to be quite female, which is most definitely my preference."

Marian cocked her head to one side. "Thank you. I was told by the ex-from-hell that I was mannish."

"You're butch—there is a big difference. At least to me." Marian was so close Liddy could smell the aroma of her shampoo.

"That doesn't put you off?" Marian's gaze wavered with uncertainty.

Damn, Liddy thought. How badly had this ex hurt Marian? She was deliciously, gently butch and obviously someone had stomped on the idea that this was attractive.

Marian closed her eyes as if she'd realized she was revealing too much. "Sorry—"

"It turns me on, if you want the truth. You're very female." Her gaze swept over Marian's curves, and she swallowed hard. "Very female, *and* you're butch, right down to those buffed nails and the comb in your back pocket." She couldn't bring herself to admit that looking at those neatly manicured nails made her consider the slenderness of Marian's fingers.

"Oh." Marian blinked rapidly, then finally looked up. "That's probably the nicest thing anyone's said to me in a long while. Okay. I forgive you for the crack about pretending we're guys."

"Thanks. My mouth got ahead of my brain with that one." *I want to go to bed with her,* Liddy thought. *Right now. Soon. Maybe in the car. I don't know—I wasn't looking. What the hell do I do now? I want to fuck Marian the Librarian from Iowa fucking City.*

Marian looked up at her, her eyes soft but serious. "What are you thinking? And don't tell me cornfields."

"That I don't know what to do." She lifted the hem of Marian's T-shirt with one fingertip. "Last time I fell into bed with someone I got hurt too. And I can't tell if how I feel right now is different from then, or if I just want it to be different."

Marian nodded. "I think it would be a mistake to go to any other level. Right now."

Liddy took a deep breath and slowly let it out. "It occurs to me if we keep talking about sex we'll eventually stop wanting to have it."

Marian's smile was crooked. "Is that the way it works?"

"So I've been told."

"Then maybe we should talk about it lots. Because it would be a big mistake for me. I'm a mess."

No kidding, Liddy wanted to say, but she caught herself. *And I thought I was a mess, getting so angry all the time.* "Well, I'm two thousand miles from home because I'm not okay either."

"So . . . shall we finish our walk?"

"Yeah," Liddy said.

She really didn't mean to grab Marian then, but her hands were on Marian's shoulders before her brain even realized what she was going to do. She pulled Marian's wonderful body close. She half expected to get slapped, though Marian hardly seemed the slapping type. She certainly thought she'd get pushed away.

Marian's arms were around her waist and their lips met hungrily. There was no teasing in this kiss. It was about yes, an ocean of yes, enough to drown in.

Marian's moan was caught in Liddy's mouth, hot and eager. Liddy could only kiss her back, no longer able to worry or think or even concentrate. She forgot about Iowa and libraries and very good reasons to stop. There was only Marian and her incredible mouth and that body that fit so well against her own.

Liddy didn't think she was the one who pulled back. Her hands were under Marian's shirt, cupping her waist. The world seemed to spin and it was a minute before she realized one of the things holding her up was Marian's thigh and hip between her legs.

"I'm sorry." Liddy shivered with the effort to separate herself from Marian, especially the hard thigh rocking slightly against her. "Sorry. I shouldn't have done that."

Marian held her a moment longer, then let her go. Liddy didn't move until Marian stepped back. "If I hadn't wanted you to I would have stopped you."

Stunned by how much she wanted to go back to what they'd been doing, Liddy said the first thing that came into her head. "We can't be alone."

"No." Marian turned away. "It would probably be for the best if we weren't."

How can she just walk away? Liddy angrily watched Marian's steady steps, yet she was also relieved. *How can she look as if she wasn't just about to do me?* And then Liddy felt a rush of hurt because she wanted to be alone with Marian again. Wanted to hold her. Wanted to smell her hair. Wanted to listen to her talk about gopher butts or tree genealogies—anything at all. Anything. And Marian was just walking away.

"Wait up!"

Marian paused. As Liddy caught up she saw that Marian was wiping away tears.

I can't, she thought. I can't hold her this time. Look where that got us.

"I don't like . . ." Marian paused to dab at her eyes. "I don't like admitting I'm not in control. I think that going to bed with you would be a huge mistake. And I want to so much that I can hardly breathe. And this isn't *like* me. It isn't. You have no idea."

Liddy realized only then that the tears had nothing to do with her. "I'm not going to bed with you," she said firmly. "If kissing you makes you cry then I'm not prepared for what will happen if I fuck you."

Marian turned toward Liddy so quickly that Liddy stepped back. "Nobody's asking to get fucked, okay? How many times do I have to say it?"

"You say it and then you kiss me."

"You kissed me! And this is childish. I don't—I don't do this. Okay, there's a lot about me I'd change if I had the chance, and I'd be better off, but this at least I know isn't me!" Her voice rose. "And I don't want to be this way. Everyone else can change, but I don't want to, thank you. I am who I am and—and—damn!" Marian turned quickly away as a group of hikers appeared at the top of the crest.

Liddy waited for the group to pass them, but all she could think was that she had no idea what was going on inside Marian. No idea at all.

Marian's low voice cut into her circular musings. "That wasn't about you. I apologize for shouting."

"Maybe we should go back now."

Marian nodded. "It's for the best."

Liddy trailed along behind her, bemused. What was it about this woman? It was those kisses. And that ass. And that voice. And the way she looked deep inside Liddy, like nobody had ever looked at her before.

Life is twisted, Liddy thought. I finally find a woman who isn't reduced to Neanderthal tactics by my boobs, but everything else about me makes her cry.

Was she in a foreign movie with no subtitles? Or was this just the way the dykes dated in Iowa City? Yes, no, yes, no, talk, talk, and more talk?

8

Eric eyed Marian as she joined him at the reference desk. "Get lucky?"

"Oh, yeah." Marian slid into one of the two vacant chairs at the reference desk. "You know me—women, women, women."

"Right." Eric's obvious disbelief was a relief, but Marian was oddly peeved by it.

So what else is new, she thought. So far today you've been angry, surrounded by sausage, laughed, kissed, turned on beyond belief, kissed more, cried pathetically and shouted at a stranger.

Liddy was hardly a stranger any longer, Inner Slut pronounced. Not if you wanted her hand down your pants.

She is a stranger, Inner Prude argued back. Why, we don't even know if she prefers milk chocolate or dark!

I'm losing it, Marian thought. Having gotten her period she could hardly blame the mood swings on hormones.

"Holy cow," Eric said. "Look who's here."

Marian watched the similarly dressed young men—neither of whom could be older than she was—walk without invitation or hesitation into Mary Jane's office. Through the dark glass she saw Mary Jane put down the phone and rise. "Oh, joy. That's what this day needed. The F.B.I."

"I wonder which of our patrons is plotting the overthrow of the government today?"

"Be nice if it was the blonde with the bad attitude, wouldn't it?"

Bill the Boor emerged from the work area behind their desk. "The F.B.I. is here?"

Marian told herself if she didn't look at him he wasn't real. That plan was foiled by the need to speak to him. "Can I sign you out of your e-mail?"

"I was about to finish up."

Marian yielded the chair and gestured at the third terminal. "Can I close the browser you've got open on this one?"

"Oh, I suppose," Bill said irritably.

"One per customer." Eric spoke cheerfully, which Marian knew made Bill even more sullen. Abruptly all business, Eric said, "Heads up."

Mary Jane's managerial mask was firmly in place. "Marian, could you join me in my office?"

Since Mary Jane hadn't mentioned the two agents there Marian wondered if they were invoking the Patriot Act. She certainly hoped not. They hadn't yet had the law enforced in their library system. Well, as far as she knew, they hadn't. Since it imposed a gag order on everyone, there was no way of knowing if it had or hadn't been applied. Beware of government conducted in secrecy, she reminded herself.

Mary Jane introduced her, explained that she had looked at their subpoena and checked it with legal, then left them alone. Fortunately, the only place to sit was behind Mary Jane's desk. It was less intimidating than standing while the two men sat.

She knew her smile was stiff, but she didn't need the patronizing "There's no reason to be alarmed, Ms. Pardoo. This person is wanted for questioning only."

Marian held back a remark about dungeons or thumbscrews. She'd met a dozen agents during her tenure at the library, and all of them prided themselves for having no sense of humor.

She spelled her name, gave her home phone number and address, then peered carefully at the photograph they showed her. "I honestly can't say I recognize which patron this is. When was this taken?"

The agent in charge answered, "We're not at liberty to say. Would you remember what books he might have asked about?"

Marian gave the dark-haired man a steady look. "I must handle a hundred requests a day. Frankly I try not to remember, as I think I'd go mad." Plus what I can't remember I can't tell you, she failed to add. If a patron struck her as furtive or somehow illicit she might remember for that reason, but otherwise she had plenty of other things to do with her time and memory cells. "Perhaps one of the other staff members?"

Emotionlessly, the other agent said, "We're not at liberty to discuss who we'll be speaking with."

Patriot Act maybe, Marian thought, or maybe not. If the matter were somebody sending threatening e-mails from a library terminal, they'd be more forthcoming. They had been in the past, at least.

"He may never have spoken to me."

"He used a terminal near your desk, Ms. Pardoo."

"Yes, near the shared reference desk, but I don't watch the patrons use the computers unless they make some sort of unusual movement. Like masturbating. Though the ones who try that usually sit facing the other way."

It was a waste of energy, trying to discomfit the two men. She wasn't being deliberately unhelpful. She really didn't remember this guy, not from a blurry, black-and-white photo printed from the security camera.

She took their card and said of course she would call if she saw that particular patron again, and of course she understood she was not able to tell anyone about this or future conversations.

They gestured for Mary Jane to come back and asked her for a list of books checked out "for the date in question," in compliance with their subpoena.

Great, Marian didn't want to know when the date in question was anyway.

Relieved the agents were back in Mary Jane's care, Marian hid her smile as Mary Jane explained that the Iowa City Public Library purged patron records once texts were returned, therefore the list would be naturally incomplete at this time.

Eric looked up when she got back to the reference desk. "Have fun with the G-men?"

"What G-men?" She gave him a significant look.

"Gotcha. The F.B.I. has not been here today."

"And therefore they're not upset that our checkout records are incomplete," Marian added.

"We should be able to tell them every book every single patron has had out," Bill muttered. "Evildoers don't have a right to privacy."

"But the rest of us do. It's called the Freedom to Read, remember?" Marian wasn't going to let Bill go unchallenged. He thought he ran the place as it was. "I'll bet whoever it is was doing course research on nuclear physics and then hopped over to read the *Socialist News* or something. And here are our tax dollars at work. Today it's terrorists, but think how helpful system logs would be—if we kept them—to turn in teenagers who look up information about abortion. Or just sex—"

"I'm not sure that's a bad idea, either." Bill raised his voice to cut Marian off. "All this resistance to filters and tracking people's books makes librarians look like hysterical leftists."

"Next you'll be quoting that moron in the *National Review* who said it was time to kill all the librarians."

"It was a metaphor," Bill said scathingly.

Marian began an angry retort, but Eric's philosophical musings stopped her. "We could help spot budding lesbians by tagging any thirteen-year-old girls who looked up information on Alice from the *Brady Bunch*."

Marian snorted. "Or Martina Navratilova." She would thank Eric later for stopping her tirade. It did no good to argue with Bill. He was an information fascist at heart, an ideology absolutely contrary to his chosen career, at least in her opinion.

Bill gave Eric a sour look and pointedly turned to his terminal.

"Oh, hey," Eric said. "I forgot to tell you, Marian. National Freedom to Read Week is now National Patriot Week, but we're not allowed to tell anyone."

Marian snickered. "Eric, I simply do not think I could get through the day without you. Okay, I'll marry you."

"Thank goodness. I don't like starch in my shirts, by the way."

"Pig," she said fondly.

Saturday evening, June 7:
Long day. Strange, queer day. Not the good kind of queer.

The you-know-what was in about I have no idea. They only talked to me and I really hate that now I feel like a suspect or an accomplice. How bothersome.

I haven't thought about Robyn seriously for at least six months and now every time I think about Liddy, I remember Robyn. Every time I think about HER, I think about Liddy, and therefore about Robyn. I have lost my grip on something, but I wish to hell I knew what it was.

Liddy didn't come in for the book, gee, I wonder why. Was it my screaming at her?

Hill has not chewed my panties, and if Trombone has thrown up, I haven't found it yet. Everything has to change all at once? A little cold cat puke would have been reassuring.

I can't stop thinking about Liddy and how close I was to unzipping her shorts.

Marian closed her journal when the doorbell rang. It was nearly nine-thirty and her eyeballs felt like someone had played beach volleyball with them and put them back unrinsed.

Amy immediately apologized. "I saw your light and I need to talk to you. Hemma's on the phone with her mom."

Too tired to be alarmed, Marian walked Amy into the kitchen and got them both cold bottled water. "I was up really early so I'm sorry if I yawn in your face, okay?"

"I know—you were stacking sausages when we saw you." Amy scooted into her favored perch on the counter. "Anyway, we talked to a realtor today and it was kind of depressing. We never finished the basement and gardens are apparently only worth it to people who want them. Not like fancy bathrooms and kitchens, which apparently are a better investment."

"I'm sorry to hear that. The garden is so wonderful."

Amy shrugged, but her eyes were full of hurt. "So we're going to get twenty-five thousand less than we thought. If we're lucky. We spent tonight talking about what to do. Hemma is all for renting it out, but we'd need a property manager. Someone who would collect the rent, fix broken stuff—"

Realizing where Amy was going, Marian said hastily, "I'd be lousy at that, even if I thought I could do it, but I'm not sure—"

"I know, that's what I told Hemma. My girl thinks you can do anything."

"I'm flattered." Marian rolled her eyes.

"That didn't come out right." Amy sipped her water. "I think you could do it, but I'm not sure you'd want to. We'd pay you a percent of the rent, of course. But I doubt that would be enough for the midnight plumbing leaks, you know? Hemma is going to ask you, and I was worried it would come out of the blue and you'd feel trapped into saying yes."

"Oh." Amy was right, she would have said yes if Hemma had asked. She was touched Amy had gone to the bother to tip her off.

Though Amy was nearly as kind and sensitive as Hemma, she showed it less. "Thanks, then. I'll think of a good excuse. Besides, renters would just destroy the garden. That's what I need, fraternity boys for neighbors."

"I wouldn't do that to you." Amy slid off the counter and drained the last of the water.

"Amy, what if you got the price the realtor said but you could sell it yourself? Wouldn't that save you a lot?"

Amy paused with her hand on the back door. "Yeah, but the market is really slow. We need the marketing help."

I'm losing my grip, Marian thought. This will never work. "I don't suppose—you don't think I could buy it, do you?" Damn Jersey for putting the idea in her head.

Amy gaped. "I didn't think you had that kind of resources."

"I don't. It's a pipe dream. I just—I sunk the settlement from my folks death into this house as a down payment and I must have some equity, though I know the market flattened out. If I could sell for even a decent price, I might be able to qualify for enough of a loan to buy yours. I love the garden." *I'd still have a piece of Hemma this way. I'd take care of the place for her. She could visit her tomatoes and tiger lilies and the apricot tree. I'd finish the basement.*

"I don't know, Marian. I would hate for business to spoil our friendship, and Hemma and I do need every penny we can get for it. We're not sure we can buy now in Hawaii. It's really expensive. We can't come down any more, though if we saved the realtor fee it would help cover the moving expenses."

"What are you looking for? I'm not going to dicker with you."

Amy told her and Marian closed her eyes to do the math in her head. "Maybe. I don't know. But tomorrow morning I'll go online and see what I could qualify for as a mortgage. At least I wouldn't kick myself forever if I really could swing it."

"We were going to list it Monday with this realtor. That is, if we weren't going to rent it out."

"Save me some pancakes and I'll drop by around ten and let you know, okay? It could be an easy answer—no way."

"Okay." Amy gave her a crooked smile. "I am going to miss you. I know Hemma's the one you're extra close to, but we're tight, too."

"Yeah." Marian was surprised that her eyes stayed dry. Maybe she was finally all cried out. "It's going to be a huge adjustment, but thank goodness for e-mail, huh?"

She locked the door behind Amy and wearily started up the stairs. But the notion wouldn't let her sleep quite yet. She trod on Hill's paw when she turned back, but he panted happily after her into the study. She found her last mortgage statement while her computer booted up, and minutes later ran a simple mortgage qualification calculator off the Web.

"Okay, Hill, if I can get a loan for that much and I sell this house for what Marva sold hers for—comparable, I think. Pay off the mortgage and I'm . . . okay. Well, that's good to know. Twenty-five thousand short. And that kind of money just grows on trees, doesn't it?" She swallowed hard while she scratched Hill's ears. Stupid idea. "When I finish my degree and get promoted I could probably swing it. But not this year. I'd have to find a Californian with more money than sense to buy this house."

California made her think of Liddy. What if it worked out somehow between them? What had she been planning to do? "Hi, come on in. Make love to me in the shrine I'm keeping for the love of my life."

Right.

"Oh, shit, Marian, don't cry." She dabbed at her eyes. "Not again."

She settled into bed, hardly able to find the energy to pull up the sheet. "Hear that, Trombone? We're going to have new neighbors. Nothing I can do about it. I told Liddy this morning that I don't like not having control over things, but this one I'll have to accept, huh?"

Unbidden, Inner Slut suggested that if she couldn't have the one Very Bad Idea of buying Hemma's house, why not give in to the Very Bad Idea of sleeping with Liddy?

"I'm bleeding," she muttered. "I can't believe she kissed me, I'm a walking oil gland." What could she possibly see in me, Marian wondered. I'm a wreck.

But Liddy had kissed her. Just before sleep washed over her, Marian was comforted by the fact that she knew where Liddy lived.

It's hard, she thought early the next morning, to think about the future before that first cup of coffee.

The paper, in a rarity of same-day relevance, predicted a storm front due in by late afternoon. That's what she needed, a thunderstorm. Maybe it would be a jolly good one. Hill hated them, but Marian liked to sit on the screened porch and listen.

"You get it, don't you, Hill? The future matters more than the past, and Hemma's the past. I'll always love her. Fuck Robyn anyway." She'd fooled herself into thinking she was in love with Robyn because she was never going to have Hemma. "It'd be rotten to do that twice in one life, wouldn't it? Some mistakes are so bad, learning from them is the only way to go on."

Hill laid his head on her feet as she pushed her mug under the coffeemaker drip.

"It's not like Liddy wants *me*. I don't know what she wants, but she can't know enough about me for it to be *me*. I'm just, I don't know, her type?" Her first thought when she'd woken up hadn't been a wish to see Hemma next to her, as she had done for years. Instead, she'd abruptly been in Liddy's arms, standing on that silly nature trail.

Mug in hand, she plodded up the stairs to pick out clothes for the day. She was tempted to get back in bed, but she needed to be semi-alert at Hemma's, and she hoped to get in an errand before then.

Thunderstorm weather. Highs in the nineties. Shorts, socks, the waterproof Jungle Mocs, a tank for the humidity, with an overshirt for the air conditioning. She sighed. Only the socks seemed to vary day-to-day. Still, she knew what she looked good in, and a new wardrobe wasn't going to change a thing. If she threw out all of her khaki shorts, she'd replace them with khaki shorts. She was actually proud of the fact that her clothes were nowhere near the tweedy baggy sweaters, long skirts and tights that made up the usual librarian chic.

"You know, Trombone, I've never seen one of those makeover shows ever take on a short butch type with—" She poked herself. "With a bit of a tummy. I think it's because they know there's no point. Not like a Dior gown is going to make me anything but a short butch type with a bit of a tummy. But I could get a haircut. Tomorrow for sure."

She watched Trombone stretch her flexible feline spine and wished idly she could do the same. It sure looked like it felt good. Perhaps she should take up yoga. Perhaps she should take up some form of exercise. Maybe exercise was better for sublimation than chocolate.

Inner Therapist reminded her that with Liddy she wouldn't have to sublimate her sex drive. Liddy was single and available, unlike a certain woman with whom Marian was *never* going to have sex. Inner Slut insisted that sex was more crucial to life than chocolate.

That slutty little voice had nothing to do with why Marian was going to Hy-Vee so early on a Sunday for a bundle of flowers and a small box of pastries. Nothing at all.

The flower selection was a little thin. She finally selected a bundle of orange-tipped carnations with a showy pale pink lily the shade of Liddy's nail polish. The pastries were harder to select. Liddy had had strawberry jam on her pancakes, but that was the only clue Marian had as to preferences. She settled for cream cheese buns topped with raspberries. Two fit perfectly in the smallest of the bakery boxes.

The greeting card aisle was her last stop and she pondered the right message. There weren't any cards that said, *Can we do it like rabbits and still be friends?* Not one read, *Ignore what I'm saying and jump me, now!* There wasn't even a cheerful *Sorry that we've had no luck arranging for a happy fuck.* She did think *Forgive me, I've been a butthead* was okay except it featured a guy with a six-pack and a real butt for a head. Not her style.

Nothing she'd seen in Liddy's house was Liddy's, so that was no help. She'd mentioned Wyeth yesterday, but none of his paintings was featured. What was the world of greeting cards coming to?

When in doubt, she thought, stick with cute. A card featuring two little girls, one wearing most of a cake on her face while the other sobbed, was blank inside, so that would work if she could think what to write.

She heard her named called and looked up to see Sandy walking toward her. "Hey, how's your dad?"

Sandy scratched her tousled hair sleepily. Marian had never seen her looking less than neatly combed and every bit of clothing pressed and tucked. "He's doing okay. But everyone is worried because he's getting weaker." She shrugged.

"Honey, how about—oh. Hey, Marian."

"Morning," Marian said to Ellie. In spite of looking as sleepy and disheveled as Sandy, Ellie had a don't-say-a-word look of warning on her face. "You two are up early," she observed mildly.

Sandy colored. "I need jelly." She hurried up the aisle. Marian realized then that she was wearing one of Ellie's T-shirts.

"Don't say it," Ellie muttered. "Just don't say it. We had dinner with her mom and when we got home it felt like old times and she's afraid her dad's gonna die and, well, we . . . just don't say it."

"You're both single."

"And getting over each other. Like we needed more breakup sex. We had plenty of that."

"Are you sure it's breakup sex?"

Ellie's eyes abruptly filled with tears. "It was too good not to be."

"I'm sorry," Marian said automatically.

Ellie shook her head, then studied the contents of Marian's cart. "Who are the flowers for? Pastries?"

"Just a sort of an 'I'm sorry' gift."

"You had a fight with Fresh Meat—Liddy—already?"

"Not exactly. I was not myself though."

"Must be serious, given how early it is."

"I've got to be at Hemma's and Amy's by ten, work at noon."

"I see."

Marian fought down a blush. She wasn't the one who'd spent the night with her ex. "Tell you what, I won't tease you if you won't tease me."

"That's hardly fun." Ellie had a masterful pout. "But okay. Deal. It's about time you got over Robyn, that shit."

"I suppose," Marian murmured. She realized she'd never been closer to telling Ellie about Hemma. But she couldn't do that standing in Hy-Vee. The sensation of being very alone and abandoned washed over her again. She felt like a defenseless child.

"Sandy was at least clear about us not being back together. Last night was just . . . old times."

Marian noticed the uncertainty in Ellie's voice. "Good thing that's all clear, huh?"

Ellie gave her a wounded look. "Stop, okay? I don't know what I'm doing here. She can't even find the apple butter. Look at her."

"I never understood what was wrong, you know? And she's just leaving us to talk."

"I never understood it either," Ellie admitted. "I just knew something wasn't right. See ya later."

Marian wrote the card while drinking a chilled Frappuccino, then drove to Deb's old house. Liddy was likely not up, so she took care to turn off the engine as soon as she was in the driveway. On the porch, though, she hesitated. Liddy would leave by the back door now that she parked behind the house. Perhaps she should put it all on the back porch.

She picked her way as quietly as possible around the house and went stealthily up the rear steps. She set down the flowers and the pastry box and tucked the card inside the flowers. Satisfied, she gave the arrangement one last pat.

The door opened.

Liddy yelped, "Holy shit, you scared me!"

Marian told herself to look up but her eyes did not want to stop gazing at Liddy's ankles, her calves, knees . . . thighs. It was a long, long journey to the hem of a faded T-shirt that was not quite long enough.

By the time she met Liddy's gaze, she was certain her skin had invented a new shade of red. "Sorry, I just wanted to be sure you saw these."

Liddy abruptly clutched the front of the T-shirt, pulling it down. "I—what are they for?"

"I was rude yesterday. I thought—"

"Oh, hell, let me put on some clothes. Come in, come in."

Marian stood awkwardly in the kitchen, cradling the flowers and not certain if she should put the pastries on the table or the counter or someplace where they wouldn't suddenly seem like a big deal.

Liddy returned with a pair of running shorts under the T-shirt and Marian abruptly felt as if there was air in the room again. She took the flowers from Marian and sniffed. "Thank you. I mean, you didn't have to."

Marian tried to slip the card into her back pocket. She hadn't wanted to be present when Liddy read it. But Liddy saw it, so she handed it over with what she hoped was a confident flourish.

"Should I read this now?"

"If you like."

"Maybe I should read it later. You meant me to find it alone."

Marian shrugged. "I do need to go. I'm having breakfast with friends and I need to be at work by noon."

Liddy cracked a sideways smile. "So I don't have to share the pastries. They look yummy."

"They are all yours."

"Nobody has ever brought me breakfast before. I mean . . . nobody who hadn't spent the night. Not that there have been that many, I mean, just . . ." Liddy sniffed the flowers appreciatively. "Thank you."

There was no air again. It had been a long time since Marian had been so aware of another woman, physically. Yes, she ached for Hemma, but she'd had years of learning to ignore it if she had to, to channel it from her moment-to-moment reality and save it for those nights at the window. All the sensible reasons she ought to channel away these feelings about Liddy were getting weak.

Instead, she let herself notice the delicate red that stained Liddy's neck now, and the unquestionable beauty of Liddy's full lips and luminous turquoise eyes. Inner Slut lingered on the long, tapered fingers tipped in short but shapely pink nails. And she could not help but notice the scent of Liddy's perfume. It was not the kind that had ever been applied from any bottle.

Seeing Liddy first thing in the morning, smiling softly, blushing mildly, left Marian feeling dizzy, weak and undeniably needy. It would only take one push to . . .

Liddy looked at her with concern. "Are you okay?"

Say something, or she'll know how bad off you are.

She might have been able to lie if Liddy's nipples hadn't hardened. She knew she was red, but it wasn't a blush. Her flush of desire was a match to the one obviously running through Liddy's body as well.

Only a few feet separated them and Marian swore her skin was trying to pull off her bones to be within reach of Liddy's fingertips. Her scalp prickled and her breasts ached to be touched. "I think I should go."

Liddy didn't move or react. There was only the rapid rise and fall of her chest, which made Marian notice how wonderfully voluptuous Liddy was. She'd never been with a woman so . . . ample. So . . . full.

Her mouth was watering.

There was no air again. All the blood in her body seemed to have drained to between her legs. For a moment she thought she might faint.

Liddy abruptly gasped for breath, breaking the taut silence. "Maybe you should. Or I'm going to start begging."

"Dear lord," Marian murmured. She turned blindly toward the door, but Liddy's voice froze her in place.

"Please. Don't go."

Had that moan come from her? Finding enough air to speak was difficult. "Liddy, I—I can't stay. We can't."

"Why not?"

"I hardly know—we don't know each other. And we both got hurt."

"I'm willing to risk it." Liddy's footsteps moved toward her. "Maybe I'm lying to myself, but I've never felt like this about anyone before."

The hot reality of Liddy's body behind her made Marian break out in a sweat. Heat and fear mingled, and her heart beat so loudly she could hardly hear her own words. "I'm still in love with someone else. It's not right for me to do that to you."

Liddy made a noise of abrupt pain, like the time Marian had caught a football with her stomach.

She whirled around to face her. "I'm sorry, Liddy. I told you I was a mess."

Her face pale as ice, Liddy said, "Yes, you should go. You really should."

"I may be a mess, but there are things I won't do, and I won't—"

"Please. Go."

There was only a long look after that, then Marian left. The back porch stairs seem to waver under her feet.

"At least I told her the truth," she said to her reflection in the rear-view mirror. "At least I remember some of the rules."

9

Liddy congratulated herself for not crying until she heard Marian's car start up. It seemed like she ought to cry because she hurt, all over. Her body had been in flames and now she felt dead. Not even angry.

She'd been the one arguing they should just give in, hadn't she? Enjoy the purely physical fun? So why did knowing that Marian was in love with someone else make all the difference in the world?

There was an empty socket where her heart ought to be. It had been that way since Robyn had ripped it out by the roots. Except looking at those flowers and the silly pastries, for a few minutes she'd felt cared for. That she mattered to someone. And if she'd had no heart she wouldn't have felt anything like that, would she? But she had.

She wanted to the throw the flowers away. Instead she put them in a pitcher she found in the cupboard. She cried over the delicious pastries and wished she wasn't eating them alone.

Marian thought *she* was a mess? She has nothing on me, Liddy thought. I'm still so mad at Robyn I could snap-kick her to Canada. It still hurts. And I'm sitting here thinking I don't need Marian to *love* me, I just want her to bring me flowers and go to bed with me and be around all the time. But not be in love with me. Right.

She finished the second pastry and made coffee. It wasn't until she'd had a relaxing few sips that she saw the card on the counter.

She wasn't sure she should read it now, but of course she did.

The picture on the front was cute, two little girls having a spat about a cake. *Dear Liddy*, she read. *I don't usually shout at new friends. I think Jane Smiley had a point, don't you? I rained on our yesterday, so I hope these brighten today. Tomorrow, who knows?*

Simple and sweet, Liddy thought, rubbing one finger over the signature. I'm a new friend. Is that what this is? Friendship? In an Iowa pig's eye, she thought.

She's in love with someone else. Friendship is what we can have.

But she sure as hell wants me, Liddy thought. The miserable ex who broke Marian's heart hadn't destroyed Marian's libido. Even if Marian still thought she was in love with the louse, she wanted Liddy as bad as Liddy wanted her.

Sooner or later, Liddy predicted, Marian will get over the nutso, and when she does—damn. I'll be in Berkeley fucking California. Home. Not here. And someone else will notice the smile, the wit, the charm and the brains. Not to mention those hips and those shoulders and that ass. If word got out what a great kisser Marian was there'd be a line around the block of the Java House. Library patronage would double. What was wrong with the dykes in this town that a woman like Marian was even single?

She sighed heavily as she finished the coffee. You're idealizing her, she told herself. Sitting here on a sugar high, smelling her flowers and thinking that she'll get over the crazy ex in time.

In time? In time for what? Before you go? Right. And then what?

Dojo, she decided, glad it was open on Sundays, and then she really needed to do more reading. Yesterday had been too unsettling.

Swear to freakin' god, she thought irritably. She wouldn't waste another day wondering about Marian the Librarian and that Mona Lisa smile and gold-green eyes that looked right into her heart. Flowers, sugar, a card—it took more than that to turn her into a pathetic, lovesick, mushy, goofy . . .

She hadn't stopped at the library to get that book, though.

Smiling slightly, she went upstairs to change.

"No, Hill, you are not going for a ride. Let's go for a walk, though. It'll be too wet tonight."

Hill danced about her for a few minutes, certain she did not really mean to take him out on the leash. She finally got him calm enough to snap it on. At the foot of the driveway she turned left, away from Hemma's and Amy's. She'd go the other way later and be in time for breakfast.

She liked her neighborhood. It wasn't as ritzy as the faculty zones, and the houses were a mix of owned and rented. But the flowerbeds were for the most part kept up and almost without fail she knew all of her neighbors by name. Hill knew every tree by smell.

The lots tended to be small, but there were exceptions. Amy and Hemma had chosen theirs precisely because it was oversized. The garden was a prize, and watching it go to someone else's care—and likely left to wither, she thought depressingly—was going to be difficult. But that was the way it was going to go.

You need to be careful, she warned herself, of making not having the house about not having Hemma. That if only you had the house, your life would not be falling apart.

Hill spotted a squirrel and barked furiously in his "Danger, danger, Will Robinson" way.

"Hill! Heel!"

After a last furious bark, Hill subsided and took up a less ferocious stance.

"Good boy, that's a good boy, protecting me from the vicious squirrel of death," Marian crooned.

"Marian!"

"Heya, Patty."

Patty mopped her brow, but kept jogging in place. "Hot as hell, but we're going to the beach later. Hopefully the storm front will hold off until tonight."

"It's supposed to be late afternoon. The beach at McBride?"

"Yeah. Maybe rent a pontoon for lunch. Wen's a little down."

"I'm sorry about that." She didn't add that Patty was looking very fit this morning. Flirting with Patty in front of Wen had always felt okay. But when they were alone, it didn't feel quite right. Like she needed another married woman in her life, she reminded herself. Patty was just plain attractive, that was all, but there was no reason to play with that particular fire. "Is the new hot tub working out?"

"Yeah. It's really great. She sleeps well after a good soak."

"You're going to die of heatstroke if you keep that up much longer."

Patty grinned. "Yeah. Okay, talk later."

"Don't forget your suntan lotion," Marian called after her. She watched Patty's trim, muscular figure lightly running away and allowed herself a brief appreciation of the view. She wasn't dead, she told herself. Noticing Patty was perfectly natural. Noticing Liddy was, too.

She'd done more than notice Liddy, Inner Slut smirked.

"Come on, Hill, stop ogling."

Hill gave her a resentful look, but Marian was content to blame everything on Hill for now.

They were greeted at home by Trombone, who told a whopping lie about how starved she was for food and attention. Hill wisely didn't brag about his walk, so there was no squabble to settle.

It was nearly ten and Marian realized she was dreading going next door. Never had she not eagerly bounded across the lawn. Maybe she was just depressed from the scene with Liddy. It was hardly a scene, she had to admit. Liddy hadn't yelled or screamed or . . . done anything remotely like Robyn. Robyn had not liked being disagreed with or her plans in any way countermanded.

Don't think about that overmuch, Inner Therapist suggested. It didn't pay to dwell on something that would surely give her a headache.

The sunlight was so sharp that it seemed impossible a storm front would be in by late afternoon. She shaded her eyes as she walked across the lawn, hoping she didn't fall apart the moment she saw Hemma.

"Hey." Hemma leaned on the doorjamb as Marian came up the front steps. "Amy said you were joining us for pancakes."

"I'm honored." She tried to find a casual air but she didn't feel the same inside. It just hurt too much to look at that gentle smile and those luminous dark eyes. Never for her—and now going away.

"Amy's got a huge stack going. I hope you're hungry."

"Yeah. I even took Hill for a walk so I could work up an appetite." She followed Hemma to the kitchen, dying with every step. How many times did she have left for the simple intimacy of a meal with Hemma—and with Amy. Family, they really were the family she had adopted when she'd moved here. Losing them both at once felt . . . bad.

Oh. She stopped for a moment, nonplussed. What day is it? June 8 . . . why was that important? Abandonment, Inner Therapist said sharply, is a familiar theme in your life, Marian. Pay attention!

"Heya, hope you're hungry!" Amy carefully transferred a yellow-corn pancake from the griddle to the platter on the table. "That's the last one." She paused halfway back to the stove. "What's wrong?"

"Sorry—"

"So am I!" Hemma threw her arms around Marian and they were crying together. Hemma's body was warm, soft . . . flush against Marian's.

Her hands trembled on Hemma's back. She wanted to touch, to feel Hemma arch slightly against her.

Not yours, she told herself. Not yours. Never was yours. It was all in your head.

"I'm so sorry, this isn't your fault. I just remembered today's the day my folks died and all of a sudden it was too much." She pushed Hemma away gently, not daring to look into her eyes. "I know that you're not going away forever. I will see you again. But . . ."

"A little close to the same nerve?"

"Yeah. I think even a marginal therapist would have spotted that one." Marian summoned a smile.

Amy waved a hand at the steaming stack of pancakes. "Food is good for the soul, you two. And it's better while it's hot."

Hemma got them both a tissue. "I feel like I'm moving away from my little sister."

Marian was glad of the tissue to cover her face for a moment. A sister, she thought. In that moment, something turned to lead inside her. What had she been doing all these years? Wanting a woman she could not have, yes, but she'd also been yearning after a woman who did not want her. A woman who would *never* want her.

Amy's pancakes were light as air and smelled of sweet corn and honeyed butter. They tasted like ash in her mouth.

"So I checked a couple of sites to see what kind of mortgage I could qualify for, and I just can't put together what you need to have. It was a lovely dream, but I just can't afford it." She sipped her water and hoped Amy didn't think her lack of appetite was the fault of the pancakes.

"I wish we could afford to loan you the money somehow," Hemma said. "But we're going to need every dime."

"It's okay." It's a decision made, Marian thought, like library school. A done deal, one to be lived with for all of the future. "I think if I went back to therapy my buying your house would easily keep me there for ten, twenty sessions."

"Why? The garden is half yours." Hemma's eyes still swam with tears.

Because building a shrine to someone who doesn't love you has got to be some sort of diagnosable disorder, Marian wanted to say.

Abandonment phobia? Just plain stupid waste of time and energy syndrome?

She adopted a gentle, reasonable tone. "Would you say that your decision to live in your friends' house was an act of denial, Marian? I think we need to explore that—oh, I see our time is up."

"Therapy isn't that bad," Amy protested.

Marian sighed. "I know. It's just . . . been there, done that. I don't need the Nice Lady once a week. I can have all the conversations on my own."

"E-mail," Hemma said. "And chat rooms, and aren't there cameras for computers now? We'll stay in touch, Marian, I promise."

A Web cam, Inner Slut mused. If they left it on, you could go on peeping.

Vexed, Marian told Inner Slut to shut up. "I know that we will. After all, if you're living in Hawaii it would be the best time to stay on your good side."

"Mercenary wretch," Hemma said fondly.

"Just remember," Amy warned. "You can't get in the door without pickled ham."

Swallowing hard, Marian nodded. She hoped it was a smile on her face. "I'll remember. You can count on it."

Sunday noon, June 8:

They're my family and I'm losing them. That explains a lot of the sudden tears and feeling so out of control. That they think of me as their family explains why HER will never love me back. I should have known that part. I didn't want to know that part.

When something gets broken, the things that were never healed become more obvious. That's why I'm thinking about Robyn. I swear my wrists ache. My shoulder hurts.

Headache looming. As if there wasn't cause enough, storm front. Work later. I hope it's a slow day.

Mom? Dad? I miss you. How would I explain what I've let happen to me? Wasting my life with unrequited love, and flirting with danger as if it was a cure? Turning my back on someone sweet and honest who at least wants me back? I wish you could meet Liddy.

Work. I really ought to call in queer.

"Yes, sensei." Liddy adjusted her stance and began the form again. Sweat poured down her back as she executed the series of punches and kicks required, then rolled into a leg sweep. Her left palm made awkward contact with the mat and she went sprawling. Fuck and fuck it. She whacked the mat as she got up.

Sensei Kerry asked, "What did the mat do to you?"

"Nothing, sensei." She resumed her stance and tried to quiet her breathing. "You could say I've had a problem with anger management."

"Had?"

"Thank you, sensei," she said, her tone very dry. "Your student is grateful for your insights."

Sensei Kerry might have laughed, but it was lost in the barked order to resume her forms practice.

She ended up on her back instead of her face, but she still wasn't rolling up to her feet. Again, again and again, until her legs wobbled and her butt ached from hitting the mat. It was a relief when the sensei sent her to practice simple kicks. She loved the satisfying thud of her foot into the practice bag.

R, she intoned with the first kick. O-B-Y-N. Robyn fucking Vaughn. Someday she would stop being angry. Maybe even today.

Maybe today she'd say good-bye forever to Robyn fucking Vaughn, and instead think about Marian. Think about being in bed with Marian. It was a much more pleasant fantasy to contemplate.

When she finally stopped she had to mop her face with her gi. She opened her eyes to see the sensei holding a towel for her. Honored, she thanked him, but he cut her off.

"Whatever it is that makes you angry, it clouds your judgment and leaves you vulnerable to indecision."

"Thank you, sensei," she said automatically. Was she being indecisive in her life? Incoherent with anger at Robyn, she'd still accepted the job, found a place to live, driven across the country and started the project.

But she hadn't been decisive with Marian, now that was true. It wasn't as if Marian made it easy, after all. Tearful one minute, the next turning on those gold-green bedroom eyes . . . Marian didn't make thinking easy. Then there was the magic she worked with her fingertips and her mouth. How did she do that?

What was it about her?

It had only been a few days, and there was obviously so much about Marian she didn't know. But the way she felt when Marian was near her was hard to argue with. It was sexual, yes, but it was more than that.

She stopped at Hy-Vee on the way home for soda and light bulbs. The bakery department still had those buns Marian had brought her. She felt stupidly nostalgic for them, though it had only been that morning. She wandered the candy aisle and found a bar of dark chocolate with raspberry filling. Given Marian's penchant, it might be wise to have some in the house.

She wished she knew where Marian lived. She'd leave the chocolate for her. She could not get through a minute without thinking about Marian and somehow she wished she could tell her so without being a fool.

She found herself looking through the greeting cards. Hmm, there didn't seem to be one that said, *Can we fuck first and talk later?* Nor one that read, *I'm not her, and you shouldn't treat me like I am. I'm not going to hurt you. I just want to make you feel good.* She sighed heavily and browsed the aisle slowly.

Marian had had pet hair on her overshirt yesterday, so she selected one with a cat and a dog sleeping peacefully side-by-side. It simply asked, *Why can't we be friends?* She'd been rude this morning, throwing Marian out like that. Well, it was true that if Marian had stayed another minute, Liddy would have touched her. The spontaneous combustion would have endangered neighboring buildings.

Back home, she surrounded herself with her books, typing notes into organized documents about women in medicine and the basics of securing a medical degree. Statistics about the teaching hospital's patient load and specialties offered mounted up rapidly. Every time she ran across a comment about medical ethics from a woman's point of view she recorded that, too. She ignored the quality-control reports themselves but recorded the labels used to describe hospital "errors." She wondered if "disadvantageous patient outcome" meant somebody had died. She'd have to find out.

Dana Moon was paying her handsomely, and she would get Liddy's best effort. At least she could do that right.

Her stomach twisted hard for food, and she realized the time. It was nearly three. Time for lunch. Time to get that book from the library, too. Maybe both errands could be accomplished at the same time. The card and chocolate she tucked into her small carryall. She'd have to be careful about the heat though.

Marian just *thought* she still loved the rotten ex, that was all. Maybe it still hurt, and she was mistaking that for a broken heart.

She showered thoroughly, moisturized every inch of her body and brushed her hair into its normal, gentle wave. No ball cap or ponytail today. Her polish would survive another couple of days. Red shorts and a simple white ribbed tank top would work for the afternoon swelter. She found a pair of twisted gold earrings, plucked a disgusting stray hair from her chin and decided she'd primped enough.

The ribbed top clung in the right places, the mirror told her. She didn't care if the rest of the world looked or not. But she'd give a lot to see those gold-green eyes pop right out of Marian's head.

Even telling herself she'd only known Marian for three days didn't calm her heartbeat. She turned the air conditioning in the

Hummer up full-blast and headed in the direction of the Pedestrian Mall.

Sunday, she thought, free parking. To her delight there were parking spaces to be had, and she nabbed one right in front of the Java House. It was a sign from above that she needed caffeine. After she locked the car she realized that Marian's Beetle, with the "I hope to be the person my dog thinks I am" bumper sticker, was parked just three spaces up. Now *that* was fortuitous. Maybe.

She placed her order and heard someone call her name.

Carrie waved an invitation to join her and two other familiar faces. She sifted through her brain. Something about mobsters . . . Jersey, she recalled. The other woman she hadn't met.

It felt, well, rather good to carry her drink over and settle into a comfortable chair, welcome to chat. Jersey and her girlfriend were holding hands. Liddy quickly learned that Terry, the girlfriend, was a veterinarian.

Jersey explained, "Terry's, like, the only dyke in I.C. I know with just one career. She doesn't even have a serious hobby."

"It doesn't leave me enough time for anything else but you, my love." Terry ran her free hand through her gray hair. Liddy idly wished that when her hair went gray it was that thick.

"Lovebirds." Carrie shrugged. "Oh, my, speaking of which."

They all followed Carrie's gaze to the counter. Ellie and Sandy were there, and they were standing very close together. Flirting, Ellie laughed and pushed her hair back. Sandy watched indulgently.

"Oh, my is right." Jersey craned her neck to see over Terry's shoulder. "Reunited?"

Terry shrugged.

"Oh, I'd say yes." Carrie seemed certain. "Their auras are very effusive with happy emotions right now. I've not seen either of them this happy in months."

"Me neither," Terry said, her voice quiet. "I didn't think Sandy would risk it again."

Ellie and Sandy joined them, but no one asked any pressing questions. Instead, Ellie grilled Liddy about Dana Moon again, and Carrie wanted to know if Liddy had ever had a homeopathic evaluation.

Questions about Dana Moon were easy to answer since she knew so little.

"We met at her agent's office so I have no idea if she really does sleep in a coffin. And no, I've never had a homeopathic evaluation," Liddy admitted.

"You have some tension in you, but your diet appears good." Carrie's bright green gaze swept over Liddy's body. Liddy wondered if this was a come-on for the holistic love couch. "While you're here I'd be happy to give you a checkup. You would be surprised what the right mix of supplements could do for you."

"I'll think about it," she said noncommittally. Tea leaves and wort of newts—her parents would be delighted if she stuck with some sort of homeopathic routine. They'd tried and failed to turn her into a true believer.

"Of course," Carrie said understandingly. She smiled warmly, but Liddy didn't sense a single ounce of sexual heat in it. Maybe she wasn't a candidate for the love couch, which would suit her just fine, even though she did wonder why she didn't qualify. How fickle was that?

Carrie turned to Sandy. "I was going to remind you about a few things I recommended, but at the moment you look remarkably healthy. Glowing, in fact."

Sandy colored and stared at her feet.

"Thank you, Dr. Carrie," Ellie said. "What would we do without you?"

"Do dykes on bikes?"

"Too much leather for me."

"Is there such a thing as too much leather?"

Liddy finished her iced coffee while Carrie and Ellie bickered. Not really wanting to join in, she instead glanced at Sandy, trying to decide how someone so quiet could mesh with a volatile woman like Ellie.

She was surprised, however, to realize that Sandy and Terry were looking at each other. Sandy shrugged ever so slightly and lowered her gaze for a moment. Terry lifted an eyebrow and gave Sandy an unmistakable inquiring look. Sandy shrugged again and then darted a glance at Jersey. This time Sandy had the inquiring look and Terry looked away.

Dyke shorthand for something, Liddy thought, but not a lingo she could translate. Carrie's moves to leave made Liddy give up trying.

"I'm off to drop some samples at Soap Opera." Carrie winked at Liddy. "Are you walking that direction?"

Liddy colored, but suddenly she didn't mind who knew she was interested in Marian. Swear to freakin' god, Liddy thought, I could get used to having friends. "Yes, as a matter of fact, I am."

Sandy and Ellie and Jersey and Terry all waved, and Liddy had an impression of an awkward silence falling as she and Carrie left.

"What's that about?" Liddy followed Carrie around the corner to the mall, dodging the ubiquitous chess game with the oversized pieces.

"Secrets," Carrie answered mysteriously. "Family secrets."

"Am I better off not knowing?"

"Depends." Carrie stepped around the falafel cart to avoid a small group enjoying a guitarist.

"On what?"

"If you're sticking around."

"Okay, I can see that." Liddy glanced at Carrie's ruddy cheeks and glowing eyes. Marian had said she was content with her life, and Liddy could see what she meant. "I don't know. We're off to a rocky start."

"You don't have to do it all in a day. Some things are better in time."

They parted ways at the fountain. Carrie turned toward Soap Opera and Liddy toward the library.

She gave herself a minute to calm down. She wanted to seem poised and confident when she saw Marian. She brushed imaginary lint off her shorts, then noticed—to her horror—that she'd missed a patch on one leg while shaving. Would Marian notice? Well, she couldn't go all the way home to fix it.

I am what I am, Marian Sue Pardoo. Liddy smoothed the tank top and made sure the scalloped edges curved evenly over her cleavage. You ain't seen nothing like me yet.

10

"That porn guy is back." Marian regarded her immediate supervisor, Dean, the head of reference, with an aggrieved air. This was the last thing her Sunday needed.

Dean gave her a weary look. "Are you sure?"

"If we wait another five minutes we'll have to dry clean the chair." She fought down a shudder. "Mary Jane's day off, and you're person-in-charge."

Dean heaved a sigh. "Same guy from last week?"

"Yeah, the middle-aged guy with the 'Shit Happens' T-shirt. He's been in magazines for a while, but he finally got a computer. Another patron has complained." Come on, Dean, she thought. Mary Jane would have had him out of here by now.

Dean finally got up and she led the way, then stood back to provide visual backup. She *hated* this. These kinds of patrons got rude and mean, sometimes, and it wasn't as if anyone ever considered that dealing with public masturbation was in a librarian's job description.

"Excuse me, sir," Dean said firmly, and just loud enough to attract the attention of the nearest patrons. "You need to stop what you're doing or I will call the police."

"Fuck off," the man snarled.

Dean turned toward the reference desk where the nearest phones were. "I am calling the police."

Cursing, the man got up. Marian noticed him pulling his hand out of his pocket. The erection was hard to miss. He stomped his way toward the exit while she quickly shut his monitor off so no other patrons would see the lurid photographs.

She was just turning to thank Dean for handling the matter when the man suddenly lunged at a reshelving cart near the lobby. "Hey!"

Her cry was lost in the sound of the books cascading to the floor as he pulled the cart onto its face. Reaching for the next one, he swore loudly and yanked it over as well.

Marian froze, horrified. Dean was already dialing 911. She was not stupid enough to try to stop him. Staff and patron safety were her only responsibilities.

"Leave him alone—please get back," Marian called to one man who looked as if he were going to interfere. "The police have been called."

Another cart crashed over as a stream of violent invectives flew, and Marian backed away. Okay, she was afraid. Eric was on the other side of the floor and two other staff members hovered worriedly at a distance. There was a rush of footsteps on the stairs from the upper floor, but thankfully no one came down. She could hear Dean describing the man as she took prudent cover behind the microfiche drawers.

All the carts tipped, the man swung around to the door, looking, Marian hoped, for escape. The door opened and to her horror a woman with a stroller and two kids came in, followed by Liddy, who had held the door.

If not for the stroller, he'd have made his way past everyone, but the stroller blocked most of the door, leaving Liddy the easiest thing to push aside. Marian was already running to help, thinking only of Liddy's tender skin and gentle fingers, of ribs that had seemed so delicate under her hands.

He swung at Liddy to get her out of his way, and Marian watched in shock as Liddy grabbed the swinging arm and propelled the heavier man into the doorjamb. The woman with the stroller yelped and grabbed at the closest of the two kids, then Marian had the other one, carrying the child away from the struggle.

She wanted to shout at Liddy that there was no telling if this guy was armed or what. She surrendered the squealing kid to the terrified mother and swung back to Liddy just in time to see her duck out of his way as he went for the door again. To Marian's immense relief, Liddy let him go.

Liddy staggered, gasping for breath. "What was that about? What happened?"

"You idiot, you didn't have to do some bullshit he-man routine!" Marian knew she was shouting, but her adrenaline was pumping too hard not to.

Liddy looked at her in astonishment. "I was just pushing him away from the kids!"

"You could have been hurt!"

"He swung at me! What was I supposed to do?"

"Is everyone okay?" Dean still had the phone in one hand, at the limit of the cord anchoring it to the wall. "Everyone is fine, no ambulance needed," he said into the handset. He listened intently, then hung up. "They've got somebody down the block they think is the guy. I'll be right back."

Marian stood gaping at Liddy, then Eric's reassuring voice carried across the floor. "It's okay, everybody, calm down. Just a little pushing and shoving. Everything is okay."

Do your job, Marian thought. She likewise began reassuring patrons, but she was aware that Liddy was stock-still, watching her. Only when it seemed that patrons were settling back down did Marian make her way to where Liddy stood.

"I'm sorry I shouted," she said in a low voice. "I was frightened."

"Me, too," Liddy whispered.

"You're okay?"

"Yeah. It was all instinct. I just pushed him away from everybody, including me. What an asshole!"

"He didn't like being told he couldn't jerk off at the library."

Male and female uniformed officers strode through the doors. Marian identified herself. Liddy admitted she was the person who had gotten into the shoving match.

The woman went to question the mother with the stroller, while the man talked to Liddy. "Did you want to press charges, ma'am?"

Liddy looked dumbfounded. "He just pushed me—"

"He's out there with a bloody nose swearing he's going to sue you."

Marian said quickly, "You should protect yourself. I'm sorry this happened, so sorry."

"I'm from California," Liddy said, as if it made all the difference.

"Yes, ma'am, but I agree with Ms. Pardoo. We can't do much about assault on books, but assault on people we can."

Liddy gave Marian a helpless look. Marian gazed back, wanting to hug her tight. Such a stupid thing. Stupid man. Stupid porn-addicted idiot of a slime bag. "I think you should."

"Okay," Liddy said to the officer. "I'll make a complaint. I mean, if that creep will do something like that with all these kids around he needs a reality check." She shrugged.

"Why don't you do the interview in the staff room," Marian suggested. She led the way, then made tea for Liddy, who looked pale. The officer accepted a glass of water, more to put Liddy at ease than anything else, Marian thought.

Dean and Eric were in a huddle with the rest of the staff over the mess of books, and Marian joined them with sorting and stacking. "Thanks, Dean, for getting the guy out of here. It's not your fault he lost it."

Dean didn't answer, but he gave her a grateful look.

Eric handed Marian a group of children's books for the stack she was setting aside. "You were great. I didn't know you could yell that loud. And you picked up that kid like he was a feather."

"I have been known to haul forty-pound bags of dirt, you know." She sighed to herself. The things she had done for love. Focus, she chided herself.

"Your friend is so butch," Eric commented.

Marian found a weak smile at the thought of Liddy's pink toenails and the impressive array of moisturizers, skin peels, hair treatments and perfumes she'd glimpsed in Liddy's bathroom—was it only two days ago? "I'll pass that on."

They were just finishing with the books when Mary Jane arrived. Dean must have called her, Marian thought. Her slacks and shirt were impeccable, but Marian caught a faint whiff of suntan lotion. This was obviously not what Mary Jane had planned to do with her day.

"Is everyone okay? What happened?" Everyone talked at once until Mary Jane shushed them. "Let's start on the incident report, Dean. Does anyone need a doctor? Did anyone break so much as a fingernail?"

"I don't think so," Dean answered. "Considering how ballistic that guy went, we were lucky."

"Except maybe Marian's friend," Eric volunteered. "He pushed her pretty hard. Course he didn't expect to get pushed back."

"Who?" Mary Jane gave Marian a piercing look.

"Liddy. She was just walking in the door as he tried to run."

"Oh, Gaia help us, is she okay?"

"I'm fine," Liddy answered for herself. Marian thought she still looked pale. "Just in the wrong place, that's all."

"Thank goodness." To Marian's surprise, Mary Jane gave Liddy a quick hug. "Did you have some tea or something?"

"Marian made me some."

Mary Jane nodded, while giving Marian a sidelong look. "Good. You're sure you're okay?"

146

"Really. I do have a brown belt," Liddy said with a tight smile. "Do you?"

Liddy shrugged. "It's mostly to stay in shape." She glanced at Marian. "I *don't* go around looking for places to pull off some he-man routine."

Ouch, Marian thought. "I am sorry about that. I may have been a bit frightened at the time."

"I came in to get that book. I didn't think . . ."

Mary Jane steadied Liddy with one hand. "Dizzy? It's just a reaction."

"I should have put sugar in the tea." Marian worried that Liddy was going to faint, but it didn't seem like a good idea to throw her arms around Liddy in front of everyone.

"This is ridiculous," Liddy muttered. "I've sparred."

"It's different when it's real."

"Marian, why don't you go ahead and take your dinner break?"

She merely nodded at Mary Jane, and then gestured toward the door and said to Liddy, "Let's get some fresh air and something to eat, okay? I could use that, seriously."

Liddy preceded her through the door and let out a surprised gasp as they stepped into the full heat of the afternoon. "Oh, I don't think I could get used to this."

"This is hot," Marian agreed. "About as bad as it gets, except for August."

"Food sounds good, all of a sudden. I had the pastries and went to work out. All I've had since is a double-shot iced mocha. And now I'm all woozy."

"We'll walk slowly."

She led Liddy down the Ped Mall toward Atlas, where the air conditioning was strong, the service good and the food cosmopolitan. A Jamaican jerk chicken burrito sounded divine.

"Does that happen a lot?"

"Never. Almost never," Marian assured her. "The most trouble we get usually is students under the influence in the evenings."

"I really wasn't trying to muscle the guy. I take karate for self-defense, sure, but the most reliable skills are the ones that let you run away."

Marian realized she was shivering as if her heart were shaking. "I really am sorry about that. I hate violence. I can't watch boxing." She didn't add that one of the worst moments of her life had been walking down the stairs and finding what Robyn had done by way of good-bye. She'd already been in so much pain, but that had been the corker. Oh, lovely—today's asshole was going to give her Robyn nightmares, she could tell.

"You're shaking," Liddy said suddenly. She stopped walking. "Honey . . . it's all over."

Her face in Liddy's shoulder, Marian had to ask if it was the brush with violence or the soft, gentle way Liddy said "honey" that made her knees wobbly. "I know."

She heard something like a giggle through Liddy's chest. "Lunch for both of us, then."

"You have to let go of me first."

"If I must."

They stared at each other for a moment, then Liddy gently patted Marian on her chest. "Not here. If we start I won't stop and we'll get heatstroke. And arrested."

Chagrined that so much showed in her face, Marian fought back the blush and led Liddy around the last corner to the restaurant.

"Oh, that feels *so* good." Liddy slid into the offered booth. "Oh, perfect, the vent is blowing right on me."

The server brought two tall glasses of iced water, then hurried away.

Liddy scanned the menu. "Sushi? I would love some California roll."

"How do you eat raw fish?"

"There's nothing raw in that. But you eat raw fish by chewing and swallowing, same as with anything else."

"Smart ass." Marian stuck out her tongue.

148

"Put that where it counts."

"You wish."

"Yeah," Liddy said seriously. "I do."

Marian sipped her water, even though her throat was abruptly too tight to swallow. "Okay, well, there were a few hours today when I wasn't Dewey, but I am now. Thanks for keeping me dehydrated."

Liddy's turquoise eyes deepened to blue. "All part of the service."

"Eric said you were so butch."

"Oh, my. Doesn't he know that just because a woman is strong it doesn't automatically make her butch?"

"He's not up on the finer aspects of it. He doesn't know you think of yourself as a Wal-Mart femme." Marian let her eyes savor the way the tank top seemed to cup Liddy's wonderful curves.

Liddy shrugged but didn't comment until after they ordered. She thanked the server then said more seriously, "I'll call myself femme, but I don't like it from other people usually. I think what I mean and they mean are two different things."

"Like what?"

"Well, what does femme mean to you?"

Marian knew the question was a test and she chose her words with care. "To me, femme is not about lipstick and nail polish, though they might be part of the package. It's a continuum. I think a femme is a woman whose femininity is on the surface, visible. So she might have nail polish." Marian reached across the table and touched her unpolished nails to Liddy's. "Or she might not. But her fingers will, to me, be unmistakably a woman's. And when she moves there would never be a doubt in my mind that she's a woman."

Liddy's face was too blank for Marian to read. "You haven't said words like 'soft' and 'pretty.'"

"I think a butch woman can be both of those things. I sometimes find the labels stifling, too. I think of myself as gently butch, but that doesn't mean I can't cry—well, you know that. It doesn't mean I can't . . . want." Damn, there was no air again.

"I know that, too," Liddy said softly. Her fingertips lightly trailed across the back of Marian's hand. "I like that you can admit it."

Trying to hide that she was panting, Marian added, "And it doesn't mean that a femme can't change a tire, either."

Liddy's laugh turned heads. "I hate those jokes. That's why I don't like being called femme, if you must know. The helpless femme jokes. They are to me no better than dumb blonde jokes."

Marian was glad Liddy moved her hand away. Her nipples were hard and she was sure it would show through the overshirt. Okay, she thought, my definition of butch means I don't like just anyone to know my nipples are hard. She glanced at Liddy. Though, she acknowledged, it looked so lovely on a woman with Liddy's endowments. "I don't care for the portrayal of butches as intimidating, angry or brooding. And sometimes emotionally stunted, or intellectually devoid. Just in the room to fuck the femme, you know?"

Liddy nodded, but she was still smiling. "I know." She shrugged. "I read those erotic anthologies—who doesn't? But I don't see myself there very often. I don't secretly pine for five butch women to work me over. As if I'm not really a femme until I've had that."

Liddy abruptly went red. Marian was delighted she knew somebody who could blush as hard as she did, though Liddy did it much less often. "What?"

"Well . . ." She sipped her water. "It's not like I haven't had that fantasy, to be honest."

Marian successfully fought back a smile. "Fantasy is safe and often not about reality."

"And mine ends with doing the housework." Liddy rolled her eyes.

"Huh?"

"No kidding—there was this one story where the play was very top and bottom, about master and a new slave and that was okay. It worked." Liddy glanced up from her plate as if to make sure the subject was okay with Marian. She smiled slightly, and continued, "But after the scene, the slave couldn't wait to show her *true* devotion by doing the dishes. Swear to freakin' god, I am *not* that kind of lesbian, thank you."

Marian said, before she could stop herself, "I don't want you to be that kind of lesbian."

Liddy gasped and didn't answer for a moment. Then, leaning forward, her voice very low, she asked, "What kind do you want me to be?"

Marian badly wanted to say, "I want you to be the kind who likes me the way I am, and I'll like you the way you are and we can just be happy forever, is that too much to ask? Oh, yeah, and don't already be married, okay?" Luckily, she was spared the need to answer by the arrival of their food.

"Try a piece—there's nothing not to like." Liddy proffered her plate of sushi rolls.

It's a rite of passage, Marian told herself. "I'm a landlubber, that's all."

"It's all cooked, nothing raw."

Seaweed, she thought, but she picked up a piece, deliberately smiled, and bit into it. Okay, I'm not gagging, was her first reaction, then she tasted the sweet and savory blend of flavors. Well, okay. "It's good. I like the hot stuff. Wasabi?"

"Yeah." Liddy's smile was pleased. "I grew up on stuff like this. My mom and dad are big health nuts."

Oh dear, Marian thought. Liddy hadn't had any of the sausages at breakfast yesterday. "Are you a vegetarian?"

"For the most part. I know all too well what red meat does to my body. Beef puts me to sleep, too."

Marian had been known to like a good steak. Frequently. Okay, so we're not a match made in heaven. This was good to know. She took a satisfying bite of her spinach and spicy chicken wrap. After swallowing she asked, "How do you feel about cats and dogs?"

"I don't think people should eat them either."

Marian snickered. "Sorry, I meant as pets."

"Oh." Liddy grinned. "You had me worried there for a moment. I like them as pets."

"Did you leave any at home when you hit the road?"

"My folks have always had cats, but I've yet to adopt any of my own."

Okay, Marian thought. That ruled out allergies. While they ate in silence for a few minutes, Marian wondered why she was asking Liddy all these questions when they weren't . . . going to do anything. Inner Slut answered that she was trying to get laid. Inner Prude objected, and Marian realized Liddy was looking at her with some concern.

"Are you okay?"

"Yeah." She grinned. "Sometimes it gets a little noisy in my head."

"Well, after that scene in the library, I guess that's understandable."

"It's got nothing to do with that," Marian said honestly. "I want you to be the kind of lesbian you want to be. What makes you happy."

"I will say one of the drawbacks of Berkeley is that everyone has a really strong opinion about how to be a lesbian." Liddy finished the last piece of her sushi roll and wiped her fingers. Marian watched in a daze as those fingers then trailed lightly along the inside of Liddy's tank top. "I'm finding it really hard to ignore what I'm thinking will make me happy." Marian didn't even have time to wonder what had happened to the oxygen in the room before Liddy added in her low, intense voice, "And that's being in your bed tonight."

Marian's head pounded in rhythm with the unending throb between her legs. Had she really been this eager, this ready, with Robyn?

"I'm sorry," Liddy said. "That was a little bald, wasn't it?"

"It's okay."

"I'm not used to just putting it right out there." She sipped her water. "I don't know what's wrong with me—"

"Or what's right?"

Liddy's smile was forced. "Could be. I don't know. I imagine people in Iowa City don't just say they want to go to bed right out in public."

"Sometimes," Marian murmured, "they do."

Liddy stared at her plate. "I'm feeling a little vulnerable here."

Belatedly, Marian said, "I want you in my bed. I want to be in your bed."

"I was worried you didn't."

"Liddy." Marian studied the top of Liddy's head and waited. When Liddy looked up, finally, Marian said quietly, but clearly, "Right now this entire room is bathed in red and I feel like I am burning. I can hardly think for wanting you. But I can't get past a couple of things."

"Like what?"

"I'm in love . . . with someone else."

"I know. I'm not asking you to be in love with me." Liddy said it firmly, but Marian saw a flicker of what might have been sadness in Liddy's eyes.

"You're leaving at the end of the summer."

"Therefore that whole falling in love thing isn't necessary, is it?"

"I got hurt last time," Marian reminded her.

"I don't want to get hurt either, so if we agree not to hurt each other—"

"And I'm not quite done with that bleeding thing."

Liddy arched an eyebrow. "Haven't you ever heard of red towels?"

Marian had to laugh. "I feel utterly unattractive from the waist down."

"That leaves me half your body to enjoy, doesn't it?"

It took a minute, but Marian found the will to breathe after she broke Liddy's intense gaze by rubbing her eyes. "You make that sound so tempting."

"I mean it to be."

If Inner Prude had anything to say, it was drowned out by Inner Slut. She's sexy and hot, Inner Slut was shouting. She wants you and you *know* you want her.

"Marian, I've been honest with you, haven't I? I left Berkeley because somebody broke my heart and damned near ruined my life. I'm breaking all the promises I made to myself before I left home. I didn't come here for an affair, but I have never wanted anybody the way I want you right now."

Was that true? Could it possibly be true, Marian wondered. Robyn had said much the same thing. That the flare of desire was meant to be. Giving in wasn't a mistake. They would make love and get to know each other. What about Hemma, Inner Prude demanded. You've loved her for years.

But I can't have her, Marian thought savagely. And she's leaving me. This morning we decided I can't buy their house. It's over. Hemma's leaving. Marian's eyes filled with unbidden tears. "I'm okay," she murmured, dabbing. "Just—a lot of emotion."

"What kinds?" Liddy looked poised to get up, but Marian couldn't tell if it was to run for the nearest exit or leap across the table and start tearing off clothes. Her entire body clenched at the thought of Liddy naked, and in her arms.

"Fear. A lot of fear."

"She really hurt you."

Marian nodded. "Yeah."

"How long ago did she leave?"

"Two years."

"Oh." Liddy was clearly speculating what kind of hurt it had been not to be healed two years later.

Ellie knew. Mary Jane knew. Of course Hemma and Amy knew, but Marian never told anyone else. Silence gives it power, she reminded herself. "We had a fight, in bed, about me not being what she wanted. Her usual shit. I was too mannish, not her type. We argued and she left. I was . . ." Her face flamed. "I was tied to the headboard and she left. She tied good knots."

154

She didn't want to tell Liddy about the hours she'd been there, struggling, her hands slowly going numb, listening to Robyn rummaging upstairs and then several places downstairs, but not knowing what Robyn was doing. Yelling for Robyn, but afraid if she did too much, her neighbors would hear. The slamming door had been a relief—at least she knew where Robyn wasn't, and she'd been afraid Robyn would come back to bed, and want to finish what they had started. She'd been helpless, for all those hours, and so afraid.

"I finally got the phone. It was just out of reach. I dislocated my shoulder, but I finally got it. Speed dial is a wonderful thing."

Liddy's expression washed over with sympathy. "That's—that's really terrible. It does give a person perspective. I thought I'd been ill-treated."

The rush of anger left Marian's head throbbing. "Glad to make you feel better."

"Oh, I'm so sorry." Liddy reached across the table to take Marian's hand. "That was thoughtless of me, really. I didn't mean it that way. I just—I understand. I really do. What a rotten, terrible thing to do. My tale of woe is nothing so bad, and I don't blame you for being scared. She so completely violated your trust."

Marian realized her pounding head was likely to turn into a migraine. The pending storm front was to blame, as well as all the stress. "I'm sorry, it's that asshole today at work, you know. Violence. It woke it all up. She never hit me, but she could have."

"You could talk to somebody about it."

"I'll put you on the long list of people who told me I should see a therapist."

"Maybe you should."

Marian shook her head. "I've done that. I know the drill. I know what it'll take and I'm not ready." Liddy didn't say anything, so Marian rushed on, "My parents were killed by a drunk driver, and three months later my brother was shot and killed in a robbery at the bank where he worked. I've *done* therapy. And then I got out of Chicago."

The color drained out of Liddy's face. "I'm sorry," she said weakly.

"So I want to go to bed with you, but I don't trust me right now. I am a *mess* right now."

Liddy spread her hands helplessly. "How can you still love that woman?"

"I don't. I'm . . . Shit." Marian dipped her fingers into her glass and rubbed her eyelids with the cool water. "My head is going to split open."

"You mean—it's someone else. Not the shitty ex."

Marian nodded, and she felt a rush of pure fear that her long-held secret was so close to the surface. "I'm going to have to get over it, because my life is on hold and has been for too long. I got a big message that I need to change it. And I'm missing out . . ." She gazed across the table at Liddy. "I'm an idiot to say no to you."

"Is that what you're doing?"

Marian thought for a minute before she answered. "I can't say yes."

Liddy's mouth twisted downward. "I'm just a victim of bad timing, is that it?"

"I didn't mean that."

Liddy dug in her pocket and came up with her wallet. She put some bills on the table and then said quietly, "Thank you for a least being honest with me."

Marian watched her walk toward the door, then lost sight of her as she disappeared into the afternoon glare.

11

What do I do now? Liddy's head was spinning.

Iowa fucking City was supposed to be quiet. Peaceful. Pastoral. Bovine. Porcine, even. Anything but wall-to-wall dykes and fisticuffs in the public library and master black belts and least of all, *least of all*, anything but home to a woman who made her feel like she was fifteen and fifty at the same time. There wasn't supposed to be a Marian the Librarian in this town who brought out such feelings of need and longing accompanied by incredible frustration.

There were other feelings, too, ones she couldn't name, but they clamored to be eased by things as simple as shared coffee in the morning and reading aloud before bed.

Swear to freakin' god, she hadn't even been here a week and all she could think about was sex and love and, damn it, Robyn Vaughn.

A voice rang out from across the mall. "Liddy!"

"Hey, Ellie." Great, she chided herself. Now I even sound like I live here.

"I heard there was a deal at the library. Mary Jane said you and Marian went for a bite to eat."

"She's at the restaurant, the one on the corner." Liddy pointed.

"Oh, Atlas. Headed home?"

"Yes. I've got piles of reading to get through."

"Seriously, if you get bored and just want to grab a bite to eat or take a break, I'd like to find out how you're doing your research. I would think research for a writer would be a fun job."

Liddy shrugged. "I haven't done enough to know, but so far, if I can keep from being distracted . . ."

Ellie grinned knowingly. "Yes, that's always the problem. Catch you later."

Liddy waved and wandered toward the Java House, where she'd left the Hummer. She didn't look down the mall toward the library. She had no reason to go in that direction. Marian wasn't there.

How does she do this to me, Liddy wondered. Lift me up so high I can't stand it? What was she going to do? She couldn't handle eight more weeks of this torture. Eight weeks isn't long enough for a lifetime, either.

The heat made her mosquito bites itch, and she remembered what Carrie had said about lavender oil. So instead of heading for her car, she continued down the mall toward Soap Opera. It had nothing to do with the library. The mist from the fountain felt wonderful. At least she wasn't so dead she couldn't enjoy that.

Poor Marian, she thought. What a hellish ex-girlfriend, to do something like that. Just . . . leave her helpless. Liddy couldn't even imagine how that would feel. Robyn had wanted to play rope games, but Liddy had always said no. Maybe her subconscious had known Robyn wasn't safe enough for that. Her refusal, though, was one of the reasons Robyn had told her she would never be a *real* femme until she'd been tied up. Bullshit, Liddy knew. Robyn had done plenty of damage, but at least it hadn't included something so insidiously physical.

She inhaled the soothing scent of sandalwood as she went into the cool store. Too dispirited to look herself, she stopped at the counter. "I'm hoping you have essential oil of lavender."

"Sure." Though this clerk was equally young, she wasn't the same one who had given Liddy the free whiff of musk. "It's made here locally, too. Wonderful fragrance."

"I'm hoping I don't smell like church linens or anything."

"Depends on how much you use. And . . ." The young woman's eyes moved slowly down Liddy's front. "And where you put it."

I don't need this, Liddy thought. "It's for mosquito bites."

"In that case, a cotton swab, just a dab."

"I'll take the small vial." She refused a sample of the musk infusion and further banter.

Bag in hand, she stood outside in the heat for a moment. The problem, she realized, wasn't Marian's past. It was the present. It was the unrequited love thing. What a waste of time. Marian at least seemed to realize it.

Great. Liddy wanted to kick the building. By the time Marian is over that, she thought, I'll be on Social Security. There was just no time for anything. There was only time for sex, exactly what Marian didn't want to have. Just sex.

Be honest, she scolded herself. You don't want it either. Not just sex. What the hell is it about her? What the hell is it about this place?

"Marian, you look like a bucket of fuck."

Marian regarded Ellie blearily. Her head felt like a truck had run over it. Her first thought had been to catch up with Liddy, but once outside the restaurant her headache had blossomed. The air was thick and heavy with the impending storm while sunlight mercilessly bored behind her eyes. She was hardly able to plod one foot in front of the other. "Thanks, I really needed to hear that right now. What exactly does a bucket of fuck look like, anyway?"

"Got a mirror?"

"Ellie, please." Standing in the sun was torture.

"Oh—migraine? Yikes, I'm sorry, I didn't realize. Where are you parked?"

"I need to go back to work."

"You need to go home sick, is what you need."

"I can take a pill. I don't want everyone to think I'm some sort of wimp." Or that she'd gone home with Liddy. Mary Jane wouldn't respect that.

"I'll walk back with you, then, okay?" Ellie could be as high-strung as a poodle sometimes, but she was never slow to nurture other people. Marian appreciated the gentle touch on the shoulder and sympathetic smile. "I wish it would just hurry up and rain. This humidity is too much. Oh, I saw Liddy. Damn, it's hot."

"Yes, she is."

Ellie burst out laughing and Marian winced, then realized what she'd said. "Sorry, I heard wrong. Was she okay?"

"Seemed it. Did you have another fight?"

"Not a fight. We just can't."

"Can't what?" Ellie dodged a skater. "She's the hottest woman I think I've seen on these old streets. If slender, feminine and built is what appeals. And it does."

"Okay, it isn't that we can't. I can't."

"Marian, you've got to be kidding."

"Ellie, please."

"You can't still be skittish because of that bitch Robyn. What she did was inexcusable, but she was a one-of-a-kind monster."

"It's not just that, it's just everything right now. Hemma . . ." This block of Ped Mall had never seemed so long.

When Marian didn't say more, Ellie said, "It's a wrench, losing them, I know. But I would think you'd welcome a romance, even if just for the summer."

"Hemma is . . ." Shit, Marian thought. I'm going to tell her. I have to tell her. "I can't buy their house. I don't have enough capital. I really wish I did."

160

"Oh, that would have been good. You love the garden." Ellie suddenly grabbed her arm. "Marian! The light's red."

Marian stepped back to the curb as a truck rumbled by. "It's for the best. I need to let go."

"They've been your family since your folks died," Ellie said softly. She gave Marian a little push when the light changed. "Hemma's the one who said you should be a librarian."

Surprised that Ellie remembered, Marian nodded. "And the books. We found the books together."

"Oh, yeah."

You're being a jerk, Marian suddenly realized. "You're my family, too, Ellie. You know that, right?"

"Yes. You're it for me. We both lost our folks young. I'm glad you decided to follow me here to I.C."

"Well, you got the place all figured out for me. It seemed like a good idea. It's worked out pretty well."

"I care about Sandy, I really do." Ellie stopped walking for a moment. "She's too good for me. Every time I fuck something up, I expect her to leave me. She never fucks up."

"You need someone a little imperfect."

Ellie smiled, but Marian could see the effort it cost her. "More than a little, if they're going to match me."

"We'll make up a list of candidates."

"I've still got the list from last year."

"Ellie? I think that any other day I'd say let's get something very cold to drink and talk it through, but my head is going to fall off. I'm sorry."

"No, I'm sorry. I do have to admit that what sounds really good to me right now is a very cold something that's blue, gets poured over ice and only tastes good with an umbrella in it."

Marian was grateful they had reached the tree-lined portion of the mall. The storm front had mercifully finally covered the sun, and it felt less humid under the trees. Just past the Java House, she thought. You can make it that far. Then she remembered she needed to get all the way back to the library. The very idea made her want to cry.

"Mary Jane!" Ellie darted to the opposite side of the mall.

By the time Marian caught up to her, Mary Jane was regarding her with concern. "I think Ellie's right, you should go home."

"Are you sure you've got coverage?"

"I'll stick around. I've got tons of paperwork to do anyway, as always."

"I'm sorry," Marian mumbled.

"Stop that. Go home and take care of yourself. That's a direct order."

Marian found a glimmer of a smile. "You top you."

Mary Jane rolled her eyes. "We'll discuss that another time."

"Thanks, El. See you."

It seemed like the longest walk of her life, but she finally reached the milestone of the Java House. And found herself face to face with Liddy, who emerged from the artist's collective next door.

"Hey."

"I'm not a stalker." Liddy flushed. "I was just browsing."

"I didn't think you were a stalker."

"But I forgot to give you this, so it's just as well."

Marian took the card. The envelope bulged with the promise of something more than paper tucked inside. "This wasn't necessary."

"I know. But I was thinking of you. Don't leave it in the sun."

"You must think I am such an idiot."

"No," Liddy said seriously. "I really don't. You keep saying you're a mess. You've got some reasons. But I don't understand why that means you have to shut me out."

"Hell, I don't understand why either. I'm so afraid."

Liddy moved closer, her voice very soft. "I'm not going to hurt you. I would never do that."

"No, you don't understand." Marian put her hand on her forehead, trying to ease the notion that her brains were going to explode out of her skull. "I'm afraid of *me*. That I'm going to hurt *you*.

Because I'm a mess and I can't promise what my feelings will be tomorrow or next week. It would kill me if I hurt you. I thought I knew myself, but these last couple of days . . ." She wanted so badly to curl up in Liddy's arms and go to sleep. Or make love. Or both. For hours and hours.

"I'm willing to give us space and time. I know this is quick. I don't even know what I'm really talking about. I'm not talking about forever, but can't we at least enjoy what we both know we're feeling?"

"It's not the sex. It's the morning after."

"Don't you think I know that? Marian . . ." Liddy's eyes sparkled with tears. "I feel like I'm struck by lightning here. It's hard to think."

Marian pointed at her head. "Migraine. And getting worse. Thinking is not my forte right now either."

"I'm sorry." Liddy cleared her throat. "Are you going to be able to get home?"

"Yes." Marian found a faint smile somehow. "I don't need any rescuing at the moment, but thank you."

They reached the Beetle and Liddy paused while Marian found her keys. "You're sure you'll get home okay?"

"Yeah. I'll take a pill and crash."

"Okay. If you're sure."

Marian nodded. Liddy didn't move on, though, so Marian looked up at her. "I'm so sorry."

"So am I."

Marian wondered if they were talking about the same thing. When Liddy stepped slightly closer and lowered her head, she knew they were.

The kiss was so gentle that Marian wanted to weep. It asked nothing of her, but felt so welcome that she caught back a whimper. Liddy must think her pathetic. So needy, so whiney, crying all the time. Wanting all the time.

She pulled back her head and took a deep breath. "I really am sorry."

Liddy did walk away then, and Marian hurt too much to cry.

163

I didn't even get the damned book, Liddy raged at herself. Another day not getting much done and she hadn't even picked up the one thing she went there for.

Like you didn't go there for her kisses, an inner voice whispered. Be honest. To look into her eyes again, that's what you were really after.

She parked the Hummer behind the house and stomped across the overgrown lawn to the back stairs. As she unlocked the door she heard the phone and dashed across the kitchen to pick it up before voice mail took over.

"Honey, I can't believe I actually got the real live you!" Her mother's warm voice was very welcome in Liddy's ear.

"Hi, Mom." What had she thought, that it would be Marian? Marian didn't even have her phone number. How could she be thinking about forever when she didn't even know where Marian lived?

"You sound blue. Are you sleeping?"

"I'm fine." Like she was going to tell her mother about Marian, right. And what the hell was there to tell? It wasn't as if a person could get a broken heart in a weekend.

"What's Iowa like?"

"Well, sort of like Fresno. Only prettier. Hills, and woods and lots of water. It's really hot, though. Not compared to Fresno, but compared to Berkeley."

"And you're eating well? Not just living on oatmeal and bananas?"

"Yes, Mom. I had sushi today."

"In Iowa?"

"I know, fooled me too. It was good." She smiled to herself. Marian's face before taking that first bite had been a picture. "I've been out to see nature and visited the libraries, and there's even a homeopath I could see if I don't feel well."

"In Iowa? They have homeopaths in Iowa?"

"Mom, there's a master sensei here in Iowa. And some excellent coffee. And running water in most homes."

Her mother's laugh was soothing over the phone line. Liddy wanted to curl up and try to explain about Marian, but it all sounded so . . . sexual. Mom had admitted that sexual heat had been the reason for her first marriage, and look how that had ended.

"Iowa City reminds me of Berkeley, actually. Not as big, but there are street musicians and vendors downtown, and people with card tables with petitions to save the spotted naked whales. Lots of rainbow flags, and plenty of peace bumper stickers. I think you'd like it."

"You're sure you're in Iowa?"

"Yes, Mom. I have the parking tickets to prove it."

"Well, that's comforting. At least I know you're running true to form. Pay them, would you, so they'll let you leave the state."

She laughed. "Yes, Mother, I will do all as you say."

They talked about Aunt Selma in Cedar Rapids. Liddy agreed to call and arrange a visit, though Aunt Selma had last seen Liddy in diapers. "So what's up with you and Daddy?"

Her mother's warm voice was so comforting. "Yesterday we got all the sets finished for a quick little play."

"Another one? You guys are manic."

"I'm Scarlet O'Hara."

Liddy giggled. "You've got the figure for it. I'll admit it even if you are my mom. But how do you have time to learn a part that big?"

"*Gone with the Wisdom* is a peace metaphor. Scarlet is just an ideal, so I have no lines. I just get to stand there with my bosoms cinched up and a price tag dangling from one ear."

"Okay." Liddy could picture the makeshift stage at one end of the park near home. She'd been to plenty of the performances of the Neighbors for Peace Troupe. "Don't hurt your bosoms. I hate it when that happens."

"Daddy sends his love and wants to know if you've sold the Hummer yet."

"No, though I've been tempted several times."

She was a little more cheerful after her mother hung up, but it quickly faded. Her documents were all stale, and words swam on the screen. It was too early to sleep.

When a clap of thunder erupted overhead, she nearly jumped out of her skin. There was an abrupt roar. It took her several seconds to realize the noise was rain pouring out of the sky.

She looked out the front windows and saw the street was quickly awash with water. Flashes of lightning had her running to turn off her laptop, and the thunder at times was so loud she thought it would break the windows.

The storm was furious and violent. It suited her mood.

Damn Marian for being a mess. And damn her rotten ex for being cruel. And damn whoever it was that Marian loved for not loving her back. And damn the rules that said no was the only answer if they didn't plan on making the Big Commitment.

Why couldn't they have yes? A simple yes, for a night full of thunder and rain?

It wasn't fair. Liddy was not used to doing without, and her body ached to have. After feeling dead for months because of Robyn fucking Vaughn, her body had woken up, and she wanted a woman with sensuous eyes, magic fingertips and fantastic kisses to take her to bed.

There was nothing wrong with that, she told herself. So how come we can only find our way to no?

Sunday afternoon, June 8:

Home sick. It's a migraine. Taking the magic pill and planning to crash. I hope I don't miss the storm though. I'm all cried out and I need rain for tears.

I want Liddy. I look back through my journals and see day after day all I could say was that I wanted HER. A day passes and I want Liddy.

I'm not fickle. I don't give up on people or dreams once I commit to them. How can I in one night say no to HER and yes to Liddy?

166

I can't. I would feel like I was cheating on HER, wouldn't I? But HER never wanted me. But I want Liddy. What a tired refrain. All I can do these days is want.

It was thunder that roused Marian after a few hours. The migraine pill had done its job. Her head was tender, but not incapacitating. A long, steamy shower felt heavenly.

"Oh, go away, Hill," she scolded. "Get your water someplace else and leave my toes alone."

It was dark out, though still two hours at least until sunset. The thunder drifted east, still rolling across the heavens but not threatening her eardrums.

She stood in the guest room doorway. The blinds were still down. On a night like tonight Hemma and Amy would be sharing a warm dinner and some quiet music. Reading or just talking. Watching them wouldn't make it her life, too.

She still didn't know why her feelings had changed about Hemma, or if it was just a temporary funk. Would she wake up tomorrow back in love again? Or was she fickle enough to fall out of love in a day?

The fantasy of their life including her, however, was well and truly gone. It had always been a fantasy, too. Though she was a dear friend, their intimacy had never included her. She'd been a bystander, and in love with the view.

She didn't want to sit home alone, wishing for company. She should call Ellie, but damn. Ellie had Sandy. At least for now.

She could play a computer game or watch TV. There was plenty to watch on Sunday nights. But concentration was difficult when her body felt so heavy and parts of her that hadn't been touched by another's hands for years were swollen.

She wanted Liddy and her body wasn't going to let her forget it. Exercise might help, but it was pouring rain.

What was a little water, she thought. A walk in the rain. The cool water and falling temperatures would soothe her head even more. She would be able to think.

She chose hiking boots as a concession to the puddles, but stayed with shorts. An old, soft T-shirt was perfect against her skin, and the waterproof windbreaker would keep part of her dry.

Hill bounded back in from the rain when she called, then shook himself dry in the kitchen. He snuffled anxiously at her jacket.

"I know it's raining, boy. It's okay, I know. Time for your dinner." On cue, Trombone twined around Marian's ankles, protesting the empty condition of her bowl. Marian was emptying the coffeepot of cold remains when she spotted the card Liddy had given her.

Raspberry-filled bittersweet chocolate. Oh, Marian thought, what a good guess. She nibbled a square and opened the card. *Why can't we be friends?* Why, indeed, she thought. Why not?

The rain had softened to a summer shower by the time she walked out into it. Puddles were deep and the air smelled faintly of ozone and wet earth. She felt good after the first block and continued on, enjoying the solitude of the streets and the sound of running water.

Another block felt fine, and then another. Sex never solved anything. It just made life harder. Why had Robyn done that to her? Left her helpless, then ruined so much? Why was anyone cruel? What had Robyn hoped to fix in herself by treating someone else so badly?

Marian no longer believed in karma. It sounded good, but if it were really true, then bad things wouldn't happen to good people. She hadn't deserved Robyn. Her brother hadn't deserved to be murdered. Her parents hadn't deserved the drunk driver.

Her feet were wet and the windbreaker hood had blown back. The rain was cooling but comforting, and she kept walking while her thoughts spun in circles.

Why had she loved Hemma? Because Hemma saw her, knew her, cared about who Marian really was. Hemma was sexy and sensuous, too, and knew how to laugh. Laughter was the best part of life, she decided. Even better than sex.

Liddy knew how to laugh. Not that she'd done much of it around Marian after the first few conversations. All she'd done for Liddy was take away the laughter. She couldn't use Liddy to forget Hemma. She couldn't go to Liddy with Hemma still in her head, or her heart. If she did it would only be sex, and there was no future in that.

She wanted some kind of future with Liddy. Any kind, except being what Liddy would regret as a "long story, but it's not going to happen again."

Rain dripped in her ears and she scrubbed her eyes with the cool water to ease the stinging of salt. At least the migraine was gone. Her legs were beginning to tire, but movement felt good. The rain was purifying.

When she stopped, finally, she knew this had been her destination all along. There was a light on and she made her way up the steps.

She rang the bell and stood dripping on the porch, certain she was going to have a very long walk home.

Liddy was still wearing that amazing, clinging tank top. She stared at Marian through the screen door, then opened it. "You're all wet."

"Well, not all of me, but quite a bit."

Liddy closed the door behind her and they stared at each other.

"Swear to freakin' god," Liddy murmured.

It was Liddy who took the step necessary, but Marian who opened her arms.

If it had been meant to be a hug, it failed completely. Their mouths met hungrily and Marian pulled Liddy's hips against her own. Their kiss was immediate union, lips, tongues, moans, air, mingling instantly, as if they had never stopped making love to each other.

Liddy's cheeks were quickly wet with rain from Marian's hair. Marian felt the drops against her hands as she cupped Liddy's face and kissed her again, and again, tasting her mouth. She rubbed her lips against Liddy's and heard, for the first time in years, her name whispered in wonder.

She licked the line of Liddy's jaw, then nipped her earlobe. And felt Liddy's body stiffen in her arms, then arch in a curve of offering.

"Marian . . ."

"Yes, darling. Yes."

The water from her windbreaker had soaked Liddy's tank top, and Marian nearly lost control at the reality of Liddy's beautiful body. She wanted to reach for what was so prominent, but she could wait. She was willing to bet that every lover before her had started there. That hardly mattered, though. She wanted to make love to all of Liddy, from the inside out.

"I hope," she whispered in Liddy's ear, "that you like lots of fore-play."

"I don't need it right now."

"I know. But I think I do."

Liddy nodded. Her voice was breathless and tight. "I can under-stand that. But don't think I'll make it easy on you." Without break-ing the long, intimate gaze, Liddy pushed down her shorts.

Marian gasped as Liddy's dark tangle of hair emerged into the light. She was so beautiful, so female. So lovely.

"Touch me, Marian. Please."

Marian could only nod. She was stunned by Liddy's surrender, and any illusion she had that she was still in control fled. She found her own kind of surrender, giving up her rationality to the moment and to the thick, hot, sweet wet that surrounded her fingertips.

Foreplay, she thought distantly. What happened to foreplay?

Liddy's back was to the door and her hips answered Marian's urgent stroking. She played in the sweetness until Liddy's knees buckled. Marian eased Liddy to the floor. She began to settle on her hip next to Liddy, but Liddy pulled Marian urgently on top of her.

Water streamed off her clothes and warmed on Liddy's body. There were too many clothes in the way, Marian realized, but her fingers wouldn't stop their exploration. Liddy moaned and opened her eyes.

Falling into turquoise, Marian held Liddy's gaze. She was stunned to realize she could read the heaving chest, the flushed arms and the vulnerable desire that reflected in Liddy's eyes. She had never felt so sure in her life of not only what was wanted, but how. "Yes, yes, look at me. Watch my face as I go inside you."

Liddy groaned and lifted her hips. One hand cupped Marian's head, twining in her hair, while the other reached down to grasp Marian's wrist. "Yes . . . Marian, please."

Liddy was dancing against her, a sensuous, rolling wave of passion. Her moan of desire turned to a gasp as Marian's fingers slid slowly inward, exploring and pleasuring.

It felt so good to have a woman moving against her like this. It had been too long. It wasn't the time to compare. There was no time to think about anything but the shudder that ran through Liddy's body and the shock that abruptly showed in Liddy's face.

"Marian! Don't stop—"

"I won't—"

"More, more—"

The grip on her hair was painful, but perversely pleasurable, and Marian felt her own body tighten and clench as Liddy froze against her. Nothing moved except what Marian stroked with her fingertips. Silken flesh shuddered there, and then everything was so wet and so tight.

They weren't words from any dictionary, but Marian knew what Liddy's incoherent words of ecstasy and climax meant. Then Liddy stopped breathing and arched again, her body straining hard against Marian's hand.

Only when Liddy finally sobbed for air did Marian find she could breathe again, too. She took her hand away just long enough to get out of the windbreaker, then she touched Liddy again. So wet, so open.

"Oh, Marian, I can't . . . yes . . ." Liddy's hips moved and the hand in Marian's hair pulled Marian's mouth down to her breasts.

Lush and firm, Marian rested her forehead on them for a moment. The wet cotton was cool. Then her teeth found one erect nipple that begged to be noticed, and Liddy groaned in response.

Marian reveled in the intricate ripples and folds between Liddy's legs while her mouth drew another gasping moan out of Liddy's throat. She could do this all night, enjoy the feel of Liddy's rolling body against her all night.

Waves on the ocean, peaking and falling only to crest again, and so wet. So very wet.

"I can't again . . . oh, yes . . . touch me like that . . ."

They left the floor eventually. Found towels, found the bed, found each other. Found their yes, hours of yes.

12

Liddy stirred against the arms around her.

Marian, she thought. She was in Marian's arms. It felt so good.

In the gray light of very early morning, she could see the circles under Marian's eyes as she slept. They were proof of Marian's vulnerability, Liddy thought. A strong woman who still felt her own tears.

She was tempted to slip away, nearly to give into the desire to be alone to think. Last night—nothing in her life had been like last night.

How could she want more, she wondered. She remembered being on top of Marian, grinding against Marian's palm, and telling Marian what she liked, how she liked it. She gave Marian every key to loving her, and Marian had used them all.

I ought to be sore. I ought to be satisfied.

Part of her was unquestionably satisfied. But that kind of completion had never happened to her before. She liked it. She wanted to feel it again.

She felt shy for being so greedy, but Marian had gasped in her ear, over and over, how much she loved what she was doing to Liddy.

Other lovers had told her she was beautiful to get her into bed.

Marian had told her she was beautiful when her body was covered in sweat, hair tangled, skin mottled with exertion and passion.

She'd been nearly asleep at one point, and Marian's magic fingertips had gently played with her hypersensitized nipples, then again between her legs until she climaxed again.

She had never . . . so many times.

She kissed Marian's forehead tenderly. Breathing hard, she nuzzled Marian's mouth and felt it come alive. Marian's hands went to Liddy's hips and then it seemed like it wasn't the morning after, just a continuation of the night.

She had meant to make love to Marian, but found herself on her back, again, tasting Marian's name in her mouth as Marian's slender, sensitive hand slipped between her thighs.

"Good morning," Marian murmured some time later.

"Hi." For a long while, all Liddy could think about was breathing.

"Be right back."

She missed Marian's warmth, but a visit to the bathroom was necessary for her too. Her mouth was so dry. Small wonder.

Marian returned with a full glass of water in her hand. "You must be thirsty."

Liddy grinned. "You think?" She gulped nearly half the glass without stopping. "Okay, my turn for a break."

With all her other lovers she had felt shy the morning after, not wanting to be naked in front of them no matter what they had done the night before. Robyn had complained that Liddy was always covering up. Guys had mostly asked that she leave her top off at least.

174

She didn't feel that way with Marian. Naked felt wonderful, and Marian's gaze following her movements was very welcome. It seemed silly to close the bathroom door.

A few minutes later she was rinsing her mouth with a dollop of toothpaste on her finger, and aware that Marian was watching her from the doorway. She'd donned her T-shirt, but it no longer hid the generous female attributes Liddy knew were there. Marian liked her breasts touched, Liddy knew that much. Their gaze met in the mirror and the intimate smile turned from sweet to heated in a matter of moments.

"I don't believe this," Liddy muttered. She washed her suddenly shaking hands.

"Believe what?" Marian slowly moved behind her and Liddy broke out in a sweat when one hand lazily caressed her lower back.

"I can't believe the way you make me feel."

"You let me in and let yourself feel it," Marian murmured.

In the mirror, Liddy could see her chest and shoulders reddening with a sexual flush in response to the intimate look in Marian's eyes. Chagrined, she splashed water on her face, then let out a choking gasp as Marian's hand sensuously caressed her ass.

She gripped the sink as Marian's fingers slipped again through all the wetness and went inside her. She moaned helplessly when the other hand found and gently pulled one nipple. "Oh, Marian, I can't . . ."

She could. She nearly fell, but somehow she stayed standing as Marian bent over her, whispering, "That's right, Liddy Emma Peel, come for me one more time."

Marian helped her to stand upright again, then turned her around. The embrace and kiss wasn't for cooling down, but heating up. Kisses so deep and sensuous that Liddy arched against Marian's pelvis in a dance of sexual abandon. Never in her life had she been like this, not with anyone. She didn't want it to ever stop and she had no idea how much more her body could take.

Marian reached behind her to turn off the forgotten tap, then pushed Liddy up onto the counter. Standing between her legs, rocking slowly, she whispered, "I like fucking you."

"I'm glad. It makes it all so much easier that you like it." Liddy gasped. "Oh . . . Marian, yes, touch me again."

Marian's fingertips were unbelievably sensitive, pressing firmly, then retreating to tease. How could she know with such certainty when Liddy wanted what? How did she know it was time . . . to go inside . . .

"Yes, sweetheart, one more time. Feel me inside you and let go."

Their mouths met for a deep kiss and Liddy felt Marian trembling. "Do you want me to? Come for you again?"

"Yes, please. *Please.*"

It had only been a few minutes since the last one. It ought to have been impossible. But the ragged plea in Marian's voice unlocked any last door to Liddy's mind and body and she cried out, thrusting herself again and again against Marian and reveling in the moans that Marian breathed into her mouth.

Which way was up? Liddy wasn't sure, then decided that up would be away from Marian's shoulder.

"Liddy," Marian was saying, "I have to lie down . . . I can't . . . hold you up anymore."

Liddy raised her head, a smile hovering, but Marian wasn't smiling. Her eyes were unfocused. Her skin showed patches of red. Liddy said, "Bed, that's a good idea."

Had her migraine returned? Liddy yanked back what covers were in the way and pulled a pillow into position for Marian's head. She expected Marian to collapse so was surprised when Marian reached up, arms open.

Their bodies melted together and the kisses began again. Dizzied, Liddy resisted the impulse to roll onto her back and realized that for the first time, Marian was the one arching with more and more urgency.

"I've been so selfish," she whispered in Marian's ear. "You are an amazing lover, Marian. I have never been like that with anyone."

"Neither have I. You . . . needed. It felt wonderful to take care of you."

"And now you need, don't you?" Liddy touched her tongue to the tip of Marian's ear, then rubbed her lips along Marian's cheek and jaw. "I am not a pillow queen, Marian. I don't think you want me to be, either."

A smile flitted over Marian's mouth. "I can't say I minded your being that way last night. Not at all."

"But now . . . please, can we take off this T-shirt?"

"Yes." Marian smiled nervously but sat up enough for Liddy to pull it over her head.

"Oh, my . . . you're so beautiful," Liddy breathed.

"You don't have to do that."

"Did I say something wrong?"

"I'm not beautiful."

"Isn't beauty in the eye of the beholder?" Liddy kissed Marian's collarbone, slowly moving down Marian's body. "I like what I see. It's beautiful to me."

Liddy moved slowly on top of Marian, sensing a skittishness that could shatter the mood in a heartbeat. Their nipples brushed and they both gasped.

"I liked the way you touched me," Liddy admitted.

She felt Marian relax slightly. "That was apparent. You're very responsive. Wonderfully so."

"I mean, my breasts. You touched them . . . just right. So gently."

"They are lovely."

"I've always had a love-hate relationship with them. You made me love them last night. This morning. Thank you."

Marian swallowed noisily as Liddy kissed the underside of one breast. "You are incredibly good for my ego."

"I hope . . . to be good for more than that." Her lips closed around one nipple and she felt it harden in her mouth. Could anything be more sensuous than knowing Marian liked her touch? She gently bit down and teased, listening to Marian's ragged breathing to know when she should be less gentle or more tender.

Marian's skin was so soft. Liddy sat astride Marian's hips and let her hands roam over stomach and ribs, shoulders and breasts, always ending with a caress of Marian's nipples. It made Marian moan and move her hips under Liddy, and Liddy began to feel drunk on Marian's voice. She bent, slowly, to kiss Marian and they both gasped again as their nipples brushed.

"I may not survive," Marian murmured. "If you don't make love to me soon, I think I might have a stroke."

"Darling, I've been making love to you all along." She slid her hand between their bodies and cupped Marian's heat. Marian gave a startled gasp that was all hunger and Liddy inwardly smiled. "But you mean like this, don't you?"

"Yes."

"I love touching you, Marian. I love saying your name and feeling you against me. I want to love every part of you. I don't think I can do what you did to me—"

"That's not what I want—"

"Tell me. Help me get it right. I want to make you feel wonderful." She pressed gently with her fingers and shuddered at the explosion of silky wet that greeted them.

"Yes, like that. Kiss me, stay close to me. Don't . . . don't go."

"I'm here," Liddy said urgently. "I'm here."

She pushed carefully inside Marian, glad of her long arms that let her slowly move inward while holding Marian close. She kissed the corners of Marian's mouth, then her neck. Marian was panting and rising to meet her.

"Like that? Is this okay?"

"Yes . . . yes . . ." Marian's hands gripped her shoulders, then pulled Liddy down for a deep, hot kiss. They shared the same air, striving together while Marian grew more and more frantic.

"Here with you, darling, I'm here. Feel me."

They kissed again and one last time, then Marian pulled Liddy against the length of her body as she shuddered. Her shaking had barely subsided when she burst into tears. Before Liddy could wonder if that was a bad thing, Marian was calming down.

I made her cry. Liddy felt . . . like a goddess. She wiped the tears off Marian's cheeks, fancifully thinking she was touching diamonds with her fingertips.

Their heartbeats matched rhythms for several minutes, then Marian whispered, "Thank you, Liddy Emma Peel."

"You keep saying my whole name."

"Does that bother you?" Marian arched an eyebrow.

"You could pick one part."

"Peel is good. Very evocative."

"My dad calls my mom that when they're lovey-dovey."

Marian's shoulders rocked with laughter. "I'll avoid it. Emma. How about that?"

"What's wrong with Liddy?"

"Nothing, except I'm not sure you like it."

Liddy blinked at Marian, a bit awed by her perceptive conclusion. "You're right, I'm not sure I do either."

"Emma does roll off the tongue well, though."

"So does Marian." Liddy kissed Marian's nose. "You're okay?"

Marian's sudden smile could have lit up the Golden Gate. "Okay is for peanut butter. I am much more than okay."

"Do you . . . It occurs to me I haven't . . ." She kissed Marian, using her tongue to suggest what she would like to do.

Marian shivered. "I do like that, but I'm not like you. I will need some time."

Liddy blushed. "I'm not like me either. I have no idea how I did all that. I've never been like that. I don't know how you knew I could be."

Marian's smile was gentle. "I didn't know you couldn't be, dear Emma."

A wonderfully gooey sensation filled the pit of Liddy's stomach, then it growled loudly. "I'm starved."

"Me too."

"Breakfast?"

"What a good idea."

Liddy thought about the contents of her refrigerator. "Want to go out?"

"Why don't I make you breakfast at my place? I need to check on my critters."

Liddy was deeply pleased. Going out meant their time together might end. Besides, she was willing to bet that being seen at any local breakfast place in Iowa City was certain to make the rumor mill. They'd be the local gossip by noon. "I'd love that."

"Do you want to shower first?"

"If I can stand up. Join me?"

"I'd love to."

They stood under the hot water together, taking turns shampooing each other's hair and washing each other's back. When Marian started to run the soap over her own breasts, Liddy snatched it away.

"Please, you need help with those. Breasts get *so* filthy and yours are simply atrocious."

Marian chuckled and leaned back to allow Liddy's touch. Once the soap was rinsed away, Liddy flicked the inviting nipples with her tongue.

Laughing, she looked up at Marian. "I would really like to do this, but I find I'm more interested in the water."

Marian pulled her up for a joyous kiss. "I'm thirsty too." Her tongue licked over Liddy's lips. Liddy shivered as she recalled Marian's tongue between her legs last night. Marian made a sound that was almost a growl, then her tongue took possession of Liddy's mouth.

This can't be happening, Liddy thought. It just can't. Marian's hands gripped her waist firmly, and then the shower wall was at her back. It was like the first time, against the door. Hot, hard and explosive.

"I've got you," Marian said, when Liddy's feet slipped. "I've got you. Let it go for me."

Liddy's voice became a wail. "Fuck me, oh, don't stop." She said more, pleaded, and felt the waves of orgasm start in the small of her back.

Marian answered in a low, intense voice that cut through the sound of water and Liddy's racing heart. "I'm not going to stop, you know I won't. I *love* being inside you. Emma . . . yes . . . Emma, I've got you." Then words were lost in a frantic kiss.

Emma, Liddy mused a few minutes later, with her head still on Marian's shoulder, was obviously multi-orgasmic. Wherever the hell Emma had come from, it felt fantastic. Marian made her feel different, made her feel alive in ways she never had before. Emma was a lucky woman. She giggled.

"All right, let's dry off and get some food."

Marian directed Liddy to the house, but didn't realize until the Hummer was in the driveway that it would announce—early on a Monday morning—that she and Liddy had spent the night together. There was no way any of her friends, including Hemma and Amy, would interpret its presence any other way.

Question was, she asked herself, did she care?

She watched Liddy's lithe body climb down out of the Hummer. No, she decided, she really didn't care. Maybe sex was the best therapy of all. She had let go of Hemma. She had no idea where things were going with Liddy, but she was free to ride the rollercoaster.

"This is Professor Hill. Down! Down! Sorry." She pulled Hill off Liddy by the collar and admonished him. "You know you're not supposed to do that."

"He's a lover," Liddy said. "A Lassie dog."

"Laddie, please. Hill may be fixed, but he's still very male." Marian realized there was a three-day accumulation of dishes in the sink. She never had gotten around to vacuuming. The early-morning sunlight caught every piece of pet hair on the furniture. "So, this is home. It's the maid's decade off."

Liddy laughed. "When I want to see the house, I'll make an appointment. Right now, I'd like to see some breakfast, please."

She nearly offered ham and eggs, but remembered Liddy's diet preferences in time. "Bagels? Cream cheese? I have some beautiful early strawberries from next door. Here, let me get the dog chow."

"Everything sounds wonderful, except the dog chow."

"Smart ass."

"I try. Shall I get plates?"

"Cupboard next to the fridge."

Hill's bowl filled, Marian began assembling their small feast to the sound of his lusty crunching. "Do you like orange juice?"

"Gives me heartburn. Coffee would be good."

"Oh, you got it. What a great idea."

"Your dishes are beautiful, the way the blue washes into the red."

Marian turned to admire them with Liddy. "From my folks. Yeah, I've always liked the colors."

She sliced the strawberries into a bowl and lightly sugared them before setting out knives for cutting bagels and spreading the cheese.

With the coffee plugged in, she shook Trombone's food container and the feline sidled into the kitchen, looking suspicious of the extra two-legged creature.

"This haughty creature is Trombone, just one, not seventy-six." She grinned, but Liddy looked blank. "You know, from the musical?"

"You lost me."

"*The Music Man*."

"Oh, I've never seen it."

Strangely enough, Marian was pleased. "Good, then you can't sing the words to 'Marian the Librarian.' Ellie does that to punish me."

Liddy goggled. "Is that where that comes from? I have to admit, I did think of you that way, but it wasn't from a musical."

"Really? Where then?"

"A book. Marian the Librarian, an S and M queen. I don't remember the title, though."

"Oh!" Marian blushed. "Oh, that book by Nicholson Baker. Yes, I've had to live that one down, too."

She had the tray on the table when Trombone hopped up onto the chair Liddy was pulling out.

"Get down," Marian ordered.

After a disdainful look, Trombone peered at the chair cushion and began heaving.

"Oh, no, you don't!" Marian scooped the cat off the chair and put her in the sink where Trombone finished throwing up. "Ha! Beat you to it."

"I think I'm not wanted."

"The cat might think she runs my life, but she doesn't. She's tried that trick before. I do anything out of the ordinary and I find gifts in my shoes. Heck, I do anything at all and she pukes in my shoes. She only chooses the chairs for new people."

Liddy, at least, didn't seem put off by it. Marian pushed away the memory of Robyn's disgust at Trombone's territorial behavior. She hadn't liked the way Hill smelled either. Face it, she told herself. Robyn didn't like anything about you, that's why she chose you. It was never about you.

Liddy tucked into her food with pleasing gusto, finishing two glasses of water along with a cup of coffee.

Marian found herself grinning helplessly.

"What?" Liddy licked a bit of cream cheese from the corner of her mouth.

"You make love like you eat. With energy and appreciation."

Liddy flushed. "I could say the same thing about you. And it's also true—you fuck like you drive."

Marian laughed delightedly. She felt so good she had to warn herself against mood swings. "If you're done I'll show you the house, such as it is. I'm sorry it's such a mess."

"A neat house is a sign of sick mind, if you ask me."

"I'm glad you feel that way." Even with Liddy's assurances, her own housekeeping appalled Marian. She rarely had company, and she'd gotten lazy. The bed was unmade and the sheets were less than fresh. Towels accumulated in the bathroom had a questionable odor after several weeks. "The ongoing presence of allergens can bolster your histamine immune response. And I've got a link to a research study that proves it."

"You don't have to convince me." Liddy was grinning. "The only reason my house is clean is I've only been there a week."

Marian didn't want to talk about how long Liddy would be staying. "I really am just lazy. Of course when school starts I'll have an excuse."

"School?"

Marian explained the value of getting a second master's degree to make use of the first one. "It feels really good to have decided to become a professional librarian. Not that I'm not already. Sheepskin just makes it official."

"I hear that. What's this?" Liddy bent over a small figure on Marian's desk.

"That's the official Librarian Action Figure." Liddy gave her a look that said she didn't believe her. "Really. Press down and she will shush you." Marian demonstrated.

"Now I've seen everything." Liddy let herself be shushed twice before she pointed at the wall calendar next to the window. "Are you a Harley and leather fan?"

Marian chortled. "No, I just like to look at fellow librarians who are."

"You're kidding." Liddy peered more closely at the description. "With all those tattoos? Those are really librarians?"

"Yeah. And when they shush, you listen."

"Okay, now I've *really* seen everything."

"Wait until I show you the Leather Librarian site on the Web."

"I can hardly wait." Liddy turned from studying the calendar. "When are you going to be Ms. August?"

"It's not my style," Marian protested.

The twinkle in Liddy's eye made Marian feel breathless and dizzy. "I think you'd look great."

Blushing, Marian led the way to the stairs.

"This quilt is beautiful." Liddy touched the hanging gently.

"My mother's work."

"Lovely. You like being a librarian? I considered it, but then I found out—"

"You wouldn't get to read books all day?"

Liddy laughed. "Yeah. Something like that."

"Common misconception."

The guest room was at least tidy, albeit dusty. "You can see part of Amy and Hemma's garden from here." Marian raised the blinds. "I helped build that fountain and retaining wall. And the arbor."

"They're the ones who are moving, right? Maybe they can put visitation rights for the fountain in the sales contract."

"I wish." She was suddenly nervous. What if Liddy noticed the window opposite?

"You have a box of ruins?"

She turned from the window and realized Liddy was standing next to the box in the corner, reading the label. "From the vicious ex." She paused. "I should get rid of it."

Liddy just looked at her. "I'm so sorry it happened, Marian. I'm sorry she hurt you."

"So am I." Making up her mind, Marian began pulling tape off the box. "Ellie and Hemma helped me clean all this up, but I haven't looked at it since."

"Are you sure you want to?"

"I think I can." She pulled open the flaps and slowly lifted out the cover of *Francie to the Rescue*. She had to swallow hard. "I had a collection of old books."

Liddy took the cover and turned it over. "Where's the rest?" When Marian gestured at the box, Liddy looked inside. "Holy shit. How could someone do that? To *books*?"

"She was nuts. She knew it would hurt me."

Liddy lifted out a handful of torn pages. "This was sick."

"I didn't know what she was doing. It took a couple of hours." Marian made herself breathe through the stab of remembered pain.

"Oh. While you were—"

"Yeah. Tied to the bed."

Liddy dropped the papers and threw her arms around Marian. "That's so awful. I'm so sorry it happened. It makes me so angry to think of someone being cruel to you!"

"It's okay." Marian held Liddy for a long moment and realized it was true. "It's okay now. Well, not okay. But . . . better."

"I'm sorry that yesterday I tried to compare my rotten ex to yours. That's not appropriate, is it?" Liddy gave her a rueful look. "But I have to admit this is more along the lines of my crazy ex."

"Do you want to talk about it?"

Liddy hesitated. "I've only told my mom, and my thesis advisor had to know. It's just—she left. No word. And took my laptop, books and research notes with her. They were in her apartment and she packed up everything and left."

Marian took Liddy's hand. "There's more, though, isn't there?"

Liddy nodded. "That was bad enough. That was actually the most work to get past. I had a backup, but I lost a lot of time redoing a lot of work. No, it gets worse with the part I can't really fix."

Marian drew Liddy to the spare bed. "I'm not suggesting we lie down, but we can sit."

"Oh, I don't know. This is more comfortable." Liddy stretched out on the bed and patted it invitingly. Marian couldn't move. "What?"

She shook her head slightly. "You're so beautiful. I can't believe you trusted me that way last night."

Liddy reached for her hand. "I'll never regret a minute of it, you know. Never."

Marian eased onto the bed, feeling nervous. But she had to smile at the twin *clomp* of shoes being kicked to the floor. "So, your crazy ex."

"Yeah, well, she walked out of her teaching job. And her reason was me. She said I'd stolen money from her and threatened her. That I was a stalker, basically, the crazy one. I didn't know she'd told people that. So then I showed up at the office she shared with another prof demanding to know where she'd gone, and I was angry, and upset and not exactly pleasant about it. I didn't know they'd been sleeping together, either. I found that out later."

"Oh. So the other woman believed you were the crazy one."

"Yeah. She believed it. And told my thesis advisor to find a way to fail me, because she'd been told I was buying my research."

"Oh, wow."

"Word got around. I could never be sure which professors knew and which didn't. I thought everyone was talking about me." Liddy's sigh was deep and heartfelt. "I couldn't do anything about that. She smeared my reputation and you don't realize until that's done what it meant. I knew a lot of faculty. I had switched my major a lot."

"But you graduated."

"Yes, but that's where I got a little lucky. I finally broke down and told my thesis advisor everything. And because she knew me, she sided with me. At least, she believed that my research was my own, and the thesis was my writing."

Marian felt a small shiver run through Liddy's body. "And you were able to finish?"

"I did, and graduated. I took this job to get out of Berkeley for a while, plus it's a great job."

"Do you know I have not the least idea what you're researching?"

"Oh." Liddy raised up on one elbow. "You weren't there, that's right. You are in bed with the woman doing research for Dana Moon's next book."

Marian blinked. "Wow. Is that great or what?"

"Great." Liddy grinned. "It's like a dream come true. Getting paid to learn stuff and write it down. And then I met this incredibly hot librarian who has been very helpful to me. Very . . . very . . . good to me."

Liddy's hand cupped Marian's breast and it felt so good Marian blushed. She tried to divert the conversation while she regained her composure. "What did you want to be when you were in college?"

"A student. I could have stayed a student all my life."

Marian chuckled. "The great Zen masters insist that we are students forever. The day you die is the day you stop learning."

Liddy turned her face to Marian's throat to whisper, "I learned a lot about myself last night."

"So did I." Liddy's fingertips were making her nipple hard. Marian didn't mind that her arousal showed. She could make love to Liddy again, this very moment.

Liddy's fingers continued to tease, but her voice took on a far-away edge. "I never lost the idea that everyone was talking about me. About the student who had an affair with a teacher and ended up driving the teacher over the edge. I got two grades much lower than I expected and I had no way of proving it wasn't deserved. I'll never know if it was her or me." Liddy nestled her head against Marian's shoulder. "I was frantically trying to recreate work on my thesis. I had to buy a new computer and replace library books that she'd taken. Mom and Dad helped, but it was humiliating to have to ask them."

"Yes, I can see how that must have been hard."

"It happened so fast. We met on April Fool's Day—prophetic, huh? I was practically living with her by the end of the month. And the first of May I went to her place and the key didn't work. She was gone."

"And nothing triggered it? She just took off?"

Liddy shrugged. "We'd had a fight about sex the night before. I was always not adventurous enough. I didn't want it enough. At least, I didn't want it the way she wanted me to have it."

Marian smiled gently and kissed Liddy on the forehead. "There is nothing wrong with you in bed."

Liddy blushed. "Well, nothing wrong with you either. She was good at that, though. Making me feel like I didn't know shit about shit. Whenever we went anywhere, she made sure to introduce me as a student, even though I was weeks from my master's degree."

"It's insidious, all that belittling."

"So my key doesn't work and no one will talk to me and my thesis is gone. And some professors I thought respected me wouldn't look me in the eye anymore. And I was so angry. Angry at myself for falling into bed with her on the first date. Angry because even when I knew she was putting me down I stayed, because she was like some addictive drug. Mostly I was pissed as shit at Robyn, though. She stole something from me I can't ever get back. I thought getting out of town for the summer would help me get over it. And it has." She smiled down at Marian.

"I'm glad." Marian stroked the side of Liddy's face, then gently pulled her down. Liddy's lips were nearly on hers when Marian froze. "Wait."

"Mmm?" Liddy closed the distance and her lips softly met Marian's. "What?"

"Robyn?"

"Yeah, the lying manipulative bitch's name was Robyn."

Marian flushed with cold. It can't be, she thought. The world is not that small. There had to be lots of college professors out there named Robyn. "Robyn—Vaughn?"

Liddy sat bolt upright. "Yes. Do you know her? I'm sorry if you do—she was a bitch to me. It cost me a couple thousand dollars to replace my shit and I won't say I'm sorry!"

Liddy had been with Robyn. The thought was deeply unsettling. Marian had felt defiled after Robyn left her, and everything Robyn had touched she poisoned. And she'd touched Liddy.

"I won't listen to her being defended. It was inexcusable, what she did—"

"She's the one. Who killed my books." Breakfast threatened to turn over in her stomach.

Liddy clapped her hand to her mouth and just stared.

"Robyn Vaughn. Visiting Professor of Women's Studies. Everybody seemed to know of her or about her, but believe me, I was the only person here who *knew* her. Took me three months to figure out she was destroying me. You're smarter than I am, obviously."

Liddy shook her head as the color drained out of her face.

Marian started to laugh and once begun found she couldn't stop.

13

"You're Mary Sue. Mary Sue from Kansas City."

They sat drinking coffee at Marian's kitchen table. Liddy had finally started to cry, which had helped Marian calm down a little. "What?"

"She told me all about Mary Sue. But she said it was Kansas City. It has to be you."

"What did she say?" I shouldn't care, Marian thought. It would have all been lies.

Liddy's laugh had no mirth in it. "You were the perfect girlfriend. The perfect lover. You let her . . . play. Adventurous in bed."

"Oh, fuck," Marian muttered. She wanted to throw the coffee mug against the wall, then she just felt tired. "Look where that got me."

"Marian, it's okay." Liddy touched her hand briefly. "Don't be ashamed of that. You didn't know you couldn't trust her, that's all. I met her almost two years later and maybe some of her freaked-out shit showed more. I just didn't trust her enough yet. I thought that someday I would."

"Can you imagine—" Marian's voice broke. "Ellie had to cut the damn things off me. She'd never tied them that tight. I got scared and said no."

"She didn't go ahead . . . after you said no?"

"No," Marian said quickly. She swallowed to hide a break in her voice. "But I was terrified she would come back to bed. I couldn't have stopped her."

"What a psychopath," Liddy snapped. "I got off lucky."

"Abuse is abuse. Don't compare. It all does the same thing."

Marian could tell that Liddy was forcing the smile. "You *have* done time in therapy, haven't you?"

"Too much. I should have gone back for a booster shot, I think." She rubbed her eyes. "Will I ever get her out of my life?"

"Yes. I will, too." Liddy refilled their coffee cups.

"She really said I was perfect? That's bizarre."

"I never thought I would ever live up to Mary Sue. Mary Sue was smart, knew what she wanted from life, worked hard, was great in bed. Actually, all of that is true."

"Hah."

"It is," Liddy insisted.

"So what was her reason for leaving Mary Sue the Saint?"

"She fell in love with her next-door neighbor and broke Robyn's heart."

Marian felt the color draining out of her face. Had Robyn *known*?

"She used Mary Sue to put me down, and to excuse her own shit. Mary Sue broke her heart so Robyn got to drink a little too much, and take it out on me sometimes."

Marian remembered to exhale. Had she brought Robyn's cruelty on herself? Had Robyn really snapped because she'd guessed Marian was in love with someone else?

Liddy was chattering, but Marian couldn't take any of it in. The phone rang and she went to answer it, glad of the interruption. It was Ellie, who sounded as if she'd been crying.

Marian asked urgently, "Are you okay?"

"No . . . no, not okay."

"Where are you?"

"Um, using the pay phone at Hy-Vee."

"Do you want me to come get you?"

"No, I can drive. I'll be there in a few minutes."

Dazed, Marian stood with her hand on the phone until Liddy asked, "Is something wrong?"

"Ellie." She turned to face Liddy and then saw that her answering machine was flashing with messages. She pressed on and listened to request after request from Ellie for her to call. "Oh, hell, she's been trying to get me all night."

"Should I go?"

"I don't want you to," Marian said. "But I don't know what to expect and—"

"I'll go. She's your best friend, right?"

Marian nodded. "And she's been there for me since we were in high school together."

"I'll go. I need to work." Liddy smiled nervously.

"Can I see you tonight? Call you later?"

The smile turned brilliant. "Yeah. It would probably help if you had my number."

Marian grinned and felt lightheaded. The inner voices arguing about Robyn were still at it, but she'd ignore them for now. She wrote her own number down for Liddy, and taped Liddy's to the refrigerator. "I will call."

"Oh, I just remembered. I have my first official class tonight at the dojo."

"Then maybe I can see you after."

Liddy's voice fell to a whisper. "I'd like that."

Tempted to push Liddy onto the counter and enjoy her body again, Marian made herself instead put her hands in her pockets.

Robyn wasn't going to ruin more of her life. Robyn wouldn't prevent her from touching Liddy again. But right now Ellie needed her.

She walked Liddy to her car and risked a kiss good-bye. Time ceased to have all meaning as Liddy's mouth melted into hers. They were still making out when Ellie pulled up to the curb.

"Time for me to go." Liddy patted Marian on the chest. "If you don't call me, I won't forgive you. And I'll call you to say so."

Marian was still chuckling as she waved a last good-bye. She drew a long conscious breath after that, then turned to Ellie, who had finally gotten out of her car.

She did a double-take. Ellie's face was streaked with tears and she was wearing the clothes she'd had on yesterday morning. "Oh, honey, what is it?" She hurried down the driveway to pull Ellie into her arms.

"I slept in the car. I didn't know what to do. You weren't home. You were with her, weren't you?"

"Yes—is that what this is about?" She drew Ellie toward the house.

"No, no. Not that. Sandy—Sandy's left me. For good."

Confused, Marian said, "But . . . you'd already broken up."

"She's moving out. I didn't realize what was happening. I'm such a fool!"

They stood in the foyer while Ellie cried into Marian's shoulder. She smoothed Ellie's back and murmured comfort.

"You know what makes it worse?" Ellie pushed Marian away and stormed into the living room. "She's moving in with someone else!"

"Who?"

"You'll never guess! Someone I thought was my friend!"

"Oh, no—who?"

"Terry."

Marian had to process this new information for a minute. "But what about Jersey?"

"Even as we speak I think Jersey is probably asking herself the same fucking question. Apparently, Terry saw Sandy and me yester-

194

day and thought we were getting back together. Sandy and Terry—they slept together a month ago. Terry cheated on Jersey."

"Terry was always clear about being nonmonogamous—"

"I know that, but I don't think for a minute Jersey really believed Terry would step out on her. Until Terry went and fucked *my* girlfriend behind my back."

"Your *ex*-girlfriend, you mean."

"I don't care! They had some fantastic weekend and Terry got all hot for change and last night she takes Sandy out. Sandy gets back and they're moving in together. They're thinking about buying Amy and Hemma's house!"

"Oh, that is twisted." Marian sat down suddenly. "The dance card will never keep up with this kind of thing."

"Now what do I do? I really loved Sandy—"

"You did not and you know it. You're scared because she's leaving your life more visibly, that's all."

Ellie blinked with hurt. "Thanks. That's so supportive."

"Life is too short, Ellie. Too short to walk around thinking you'll never get what you want because somebody else has it or took it."

Ellie snapped, "Like you mooning over Hemma all these years?"

There was only the sound of Hill's claws on the kitchen floor to break the silence. Finally, feeling so heavy she could hardly make her mouth work, Marian asked, "Does everybody know?"

Ellie started to cry again. "I don't think so. Just me. You let it show sometimes, that's all."

This morning's tears welled up again, but Marian shoved them back down viciously. Enough, she thought. Enough. "I'm so sorry, El. About Sandy."

"I'm sorry about Hemma. I'm sorry I didn't say something. I was waiting for you to tell me. I know sometimes you felt so bad. But mostly you seemed happy."

"I was, mostly. But in a holding pattern."

Ellie nodded soberly. "True. But the pattern has been broken."

Marian could only agree. "I didn't want anything to change."

"I'll bet Jersey feels the same way right now."

"Jersey is going to be a mess." Marian pictured the confusion and hurt Jersey had to be feeling. She might be dense at times, but Jersey wouldn't hurt the proverbial fly. Poor thing.

Ellie blew her nose. "Hell, at least she's single. I've always been curious."

Laughter bubbled through Marian's self-pitying urge to cry. "You are incorrigible."

"I'm single and pushing forty."

"In six years."

"I should have just taken that threeway with Patty and Wen."

Marian gaped. "The *what*?"

"Oh, fuck, I never told you about that, but what the hell does it matter. You won't tell anybody."

"No, I won't." Inner Historian was dancing with glee to have yet more items for the dance card. "It sounds juicy."

Ellie shrugged and collapsed onto the sofa. She wiped her nose with her crumpled tissue. "After Wen started feeling the arthritis she got really worried she was going to lose her ability to enjoy sex."

"I wondered—she sometimes sounds wistful about it and Patty is always reassuring."

"Yeah, so, Wen did some experimenting without Patty."

"Oh. With you?"

"Yeah. We had a couple of good nights. That's when she was with Carrie, too."

"Oh. I knew they'd been together, but I didn't know when." Inner Historian made a note.

"Anyway, it really does seem foolish now that it mattered to me that Wen wanted just me. But she's in love with Patty, and didn't want to give up Patty for me. That hurt."

"So what about the threeway?" Inner Prude was busily trying to scrub out the images Inner Slut was parading through Marian's mind.

When Ellie wiped her nose again, Marian tossed a box of tissues across to the sofa.

"Thanks. Well, thing is, Wen told Patty because she felt guilty. But Patty wasn't . . . upset. She was actually really turned on by it, which I guess surprised the hell out of both of them. So they came to see me, to see if I would . . . and I said no. I was just starting to see Sandy by then."

"Wow."

"It was really awkward for a while, but then everything settled down again."

Marian opened her mouth, then closed it again. "Do you think they found somebody?"

"To play with?"

Marian nodded.

"Yeah, I do."

"Oh . . ." This *was* juicy. "Mary Jane."

"Yeah, that's what I've always thought."

Inner Prude was repelled. Inner Slut thought it sounded like a helluva good time—muscled Patty, confident Mary Jane, gentle Wen. "I hope they're having fun."

Ellie sighed. "Even you are now. Everybody is but me."

Marian sighed. "Jersey's not having any fun right now."

"I'll call her later." Ellie gave a self-deprecating laugh. "Maybe we'll just do what everyone else is doing, have a great fuck and get over it."

Marian blushed beet red.

Ellie immediately noticed. "Oh, my, speaking of great fucks, how was she?"

Marian decided to take a page from Mary Jane's book. "That would be ungallant."

"You are red as a fire truck!"

"You can't make me say, Ellie."

"That good?"

"Damn good," Marian said before she could stop herself. "I could fall in love with her."

"Aren't you already?"

197

"Maybe." Marian sighed heavily. The chair was coated in cat hair. "She's not sticking around, remember?"

"You've got some time to change her mind."

Marian allowed herself a tiny smile. "I guess so. Ellie, I've never felt this way with *anyone*. Like I had the power to make her fantasies come true."

"It's not like you can count your lovers on more than one hand, M'Sue."

"I know, but . . . it was different. I felt . . . like I was discovering who I could be with her. More than I thought."

"You know what I always say—who cares if it's forever as long as today is good."

"It's good."

"And I cut off your date. I'm sorry."

"It's okay." Marian rose. "I'm ravenous, too. Let's go get some breakfast. More breakfast for me, but I didn't have dinner last night."

"I didn't have dinner either. Hamburg Inn?"

"Everyone will think we spent the night together."

"Hell, let's give them something to talk about."

Ellie laughed, sounding happier than Marian had thought she would be for a while. "I'm glad you're my best friend, M'Sue. I don't know what I'd do without you."

"Hey," Marian began. "You'll never guess something that Liddy and I have in common. *Someone* we have in common."

"She slept with Carrie already? I thought you couldn't be with someone who'd been with an ex."

Marian led the way out the door. "Oh, you have no idea. I think I'll have to get over that because the universe is twisted."

Liddy pushed the stack of books away and rested her head on her arms. She'd had a nap, but she still felt too restless to work.

What was Marian doing? What was wrong with Ellie? Would she call before evening?

She dabbed lavender oil on her mosquito bites and, to her amazement, it worked equally as well as any anti-itch cream she'd tried. It didn't smell bad at all.

She paced. She turned the Cranberries up loud, but the music failed to distract her. Finally, she went for a drive because the Hummer had better speakers than the boom box.

Not sure she wouldn't get lost, she followed what she hoped was the route to the overlook where Marian had driven her on Saturday. The occasional landmark looked familiar, and in a short time she was parked.

She was a long way from home. Even so, Robyn Vaughn had followed her. Not Robyn, she thought suddenly. The pain Robyn caused followed you here, and here is where you'll let it go. You can get hurt again, but not by Robyn. A wave of peace washed over her, and for the first time in weeks there was no anger simmering in her heart.

It was very quiet and she stood looking down at the countryside with only a light breeze against the leaves for noise.

Female. Lush. Wet. Alive. Iowa was all those things.

So was Marian. And so was she when she was with Marian.

It's not paradise, she thought. Not quite. But it could feel like home with Marian.

"I don't know what her dreams are," Liddy said to the breeze. "I don't know all of her pain, I think. I want to know, though. I want to see behind those amazing eyes."

She hugged herself for a moment, remembering the way it had felt to be in Marian's arms. Nobody had ever touched her like that.

"Hell, I don't even know how old she is. More than thirty. But close enough. I'll catch up." She realized what she was considering and laughed aloud. "You don't have to decide today, Liddy Emma Peel."

And, she added, I want to hear her call me Emma again and feel her against me. Emma . . . Emma is for her.

After her lengthy breakfast with Ellie, Marian wanted to call Liddy. Perhaps drop by. Perhaps spend the day in bed. But Ellie was still forlorn and diversions were the duty of a best friend.

"I think I need a new outfit or something," Ellie announced.

"Are you going to make me watch you try on clothes at Von Maur?" Marian sighed as she unlocked the car.

"Yes, it's the least you can do. You've got a girlfriend and I don't."

"I'll just practice, shall I? No, that doesn't make your ass look like a house. Yes, that color is perfect with your eyes." She adopted the tone she used when humoring Trombone. "No, you are not getting old."

"Shut up."

"Can't we go to the movies instead?"

"Too transitory. I need a skirt and possibly shoes."

"With a house payment to cover on your own, maybe Von Maur isn't the place to go."

Ellie sulked. "You really know how to rain on a girl's parade, don't you?"

"It's cheaper being a Wal-Mart femme."

Ellie laughed at that and Marian turned in that direction.

After shopping came lunch—a fiesta of grease and salt from a fast-food place—and then Ellie was finally ready to go home.

"Only if you'll come with me to see who's there. I'll walk over for my car later."

"What if Sandy's there? What will you do?"

"Talk to her. Make sure she knows if Terry will leave Jersey after five years for her, Terry will eventually leave her, too."

"Probably true."

Ellie put her head back on the seat. "I taught her that lesson, you know. What am I complaining about? I don't really believe in forever after. Sandy does, so she gets more hurt than I do."

I believe in it, too, Marian wanted to say. Amy and Hemma had it. Her parents had had it. There were people who worked it out, who somehow kept it together.

She wanted to be one of those people. And she had no idea if Liddy wanted to be one, or if she felt like Ellie did, that it was an impossible dream.

Well, she thought, you'll just have to ask her, won't you?

"Oh, hell, Terry's there." Ellie ducked down in the seat.

"It had to happen sometime."

"You know, why don't we go see Jersey instead?"

Marian made a quick U-turn. "I think that's a great idea."

"Liddy!"

Liddy turned in the direction of the voice, then grinned as she lifted her freshly made latte. "Hi, Carrie. I'm addicted to this place. You all got me hooked. I couldn't concentrate and here I am for my fix. You here for yours?"

"Today's a cocoa-and-cream day," Carrie answered. "Have you heard the news about Terry and Jersey?"

"No. Nothing bad I hope."

Carrie rolled her eyes. "It depends on your perspective. Let me get my drink and I'll fill you in."

The comfy upholstered chairs were unoccupied, and Liddy quickly dropped into one. She liked this place, though her budget would start to feel the habit soon.

After a moment she wondered what was taking Carrie so long, then realized someone else had come in. What was that woman's name? Would she ever remember? Those muscles were amazing, though.

Whatever Carrie and the woman were discussing was very intense, with lots of nodding and shaking of their heads. Maybe it was about Ellie. She was starting to get frustrated with curiosity when the other woman left, two drinks in hand, and Carrie finally joined her.

"Patty had more details."

Patty. Muscles. Got it, she thought. "So what is it?"

"Well, Terry and Jersey broke up. This morning. After Terry spent the night—not for the first time is what Patty just told me—with Sandy."

Liddy had to think about it for a moment. Then she started asking questions. Carrie, as it turned out, knew a lot about a lot. Liddy's head spun keeping track of who had been with whom, in what order, where they'd lived, and who had custody of all the pets. "Does this happen a lot in Iowa City?"

"What's the definition of 'a lot'? Sometimes it does seem a little bit like square dancing. Allemande left, y'all."

Liddy laughed. She liked Carrie, but was glad she wasn't a candidate for the holistic love couch. She didn't even care why she wasn't. "I bet it upsets the stability of the group for a while."

"Oh, most assuredly, especially with those who waste their time being possessive. I try to take people as they wish to be received. It requires too much energy otherwise."

Liddy tried not to ask, but she had to. "Is this going to bother Marian?"

Carrie regarded her curiously. "Does it matter to you if it does?"

Liddy colored. "Yes."

"Marian will roll with it. She's learning. Give her time."

"I'm supposed leave at the end of July."

Carrie touched Liddy's wrist for just a moment. "I became happy when I let go of 'supposed to.'"

"You sound like Sensei Kerry."

Carrie grinned. "If you mean that wonderful man Kerry at the Golden Dragon, I'm honored."

They chatted about a variety of topics, and it was some time before Liddy realized the afternoon was slipping away. "I'm really sorry, but I should get some work done today. But I have enjoyed talking, a lot."

"So have I, dear. You're a welcome change of pace, even if you do leave us again. Say hello to Marian for me."

"How do you know I'll see her?"

Carrie abruptly looked smug. "She kicked your car. The best part is—after your happiness, of course—I win the pool."

"Pool? There was a bet on who would end up with me?"

"Horrid, isn't it?"

"Yes," Liddy said indignantly. "I think it is. I'm a woman, not a horse."

"I couldn't agree more, but it's so rare we get fresh meat in the summer that I had to join in." Carrie blinked innocently.

"Well, I'm glad you won at least." Slowly, a smile took over. "But I'm the one who really won. At least I will, if I work at it."

Jersey had been a mess, not that either Marian or Ellie found that the least bit odd. They did what they could, which was to listen and comfort her. Jersey was manically packing her things, not sure where she would go when the house was sold. An electrician could make ends meet, but how would she have time for classes if she was paying rent on her own? They'd tried to reassure her it wouldn't happen tomorrow, but Jersey was adamant she had to be ready to move at a moment's notice.

Marian wasn't sure that Ellie's offer of a place to stay was the wisest move on Ellie's part, but hell, she had enough to worry about with her own love life. They could just trade places, and maybe that would be simplest all the way around. Inner Prude could just shut up about it.

She had to go home for Liddy's number. Her stomach growled for dinner. Hill and Trombone were likewise vocal about their hunger. She took care of their needs, but skipped her own, hoping to have dinner with Liddy.

Liddy wasn't answering her home phone or her cell. Karate lesson, Marian abruptly recalled. That was tonight. Oh, hell, she thought, now Liddy will think I didn't call, and she'll worry I'm a heartless cad or something. I don't want her to worry about something like that. I'm not Robyn. Neither is she. And there is no way I am going to let Robyn Vaughn steal anything more from me, and that includes a chance to get to know Liddy.

The Internet had its uses. Marian had had no idea there were four places to learn martial arts in Iowa City, and another two in Coralville. She printed the list and decided to try the closest one. Failing that, she'd just wait at Liddy's house.

Luck was with her. The sight of the Hummer in front of the Golden Dragon Martial Arts Academy made her stomach do a little dance.

Liddy didn't notice her slipping in the door, but she had good reason. The class of roughly a dozen people was moving very quickly through moves that looked more like dance than anything else, except in dance nobody actually got kicked, swatted or knocked over.

It was mesmerizing. Liddy moved like a cat.

Marian remembered those muscles against her last night. How had she ever thought Liddy was fragile? But she was, at least on the inside, Marian reminded herself. Strong, intelligent, fragile, funny, passionate, caring—in other words, a woman. A good woman.

By the time class ended, Marian had committed every movement of Liddy's body to memory. Liddy spoke with the sensei for a few minutes, then collected a bag not far from where Marian was sitting, and hurried toward the door.

Amused, Marian followed her. Liddy was getting out her cell phone.

She nearly laughed out loud when her own phone rang. She answered, unable to keep the merriment out of her voice.

"You shit, you said you'd call."

"I'm sorry, it's been a busy day. I got caught up comforting Jersey."

"I've heard all the news. You sound way too happy without me." Liddy unlocked her car and tossed her bag in it.

"Careful with that bag, you could break something."

"What?"

"Turn around, Emma."

Liddy pivoted in place and stared. She said into the phone, "Okay, I forgive you," and hung up.

Marian meant to saunter. She then thought she could hold herself to a stroll. It became a half-run as Liddy started toward her and they collided, in the parking lot of the Golden Dragon, in plain sight of the world.

She kissed Liddy without holding anything back. It was nice to have love out in the open. She kissed Liddy again.

Liddy finally pushed her away. "I'm all sweaty."

"I like you this way. You were the first time you held me."

"Oh, you noticed."

"I think I've noticed everything about you."

"There's a lot more to know."

Marian nodded. "A lot more for me to tell." I can tell her everything as we go along, she promised herself. I think she can handle it. "Talking is good. If we stay out of bed we can talk more."

"Why can't we talk in bed?" Liddy scrubbed her face with the sleeve of her uniform. "I don't know where we're going, Marian. I'm a little scared. I'm a long way from home."

"And this isn't home." With a tiny rush of courage, Marian added, "Yet."

Liddy's shy smile reached her eyes. "I'm not saying it couldn't be."

"I'm not ready for a commitment."

Surprisingly, Liddy answered, "I am."

"Oh." Marian didn't quite know what to say to that.

"Don't panic, you nit."

"I'm not a nit!"

Liddy arched an eyebrow. "I meant that I am willing to commit to trying."

Slowly, Marian nodded. "Me, too. Yes, I can commit to that."

"We've got seven weeks," Liddy said philosophically.

"Practically forever."

Forever, Marian thought as Liddy melted into her again, might not be long enough with this woman. They swayed against each other until Liddy drew her head back with a laugh.

"We can dance someplace else, you know?"

"It's not this kind of dancing I have in mind," Marian answered. "I want a long dance with you, though, a very long dance."

Liddy caught her breath, then a slow smile crept over her face. "What do you call this dance?"

Marian laughed. "We're going to have to talk that over, I think."

"Oh, more talk." Liddy's mock pout was, Marian had to admit, adorable.

"We'll have to practice dancing, too."

"That is sounding more appealing." Liddy pulled Marian against the Hummer. "I'm ready."

"For what?" She swallowed hard as Liddy's hands slid underneath her T-shirt to stroke her back.

Liddy's answer was nearly lost under the pounding of Marian's heart.

"Everything."

Thursday evening, November 25:

Getting lazy about writing in my journal. So much to cover.

I've never had a vegetarian Thanksgiving before, but everything was tasty. Liddy's mom is a good cook. Her dad seems to like me. I'm worried they'll be cold in the guest room.

This morning L couldn't find a decent pair of panties to wear, thanks to Hill. She said her mom would know it had holes, so she opted for a skimpy thong that came with a negligee. All day that knowledge has been quite distracting.

Tickets to Hawaii are expensive, but worth it. I'm amazed that L still wants to go, after I told her about Hemma. She says she wants to be sure I'm over it, and that I'm not just calling her Emma to cover! I've taken to enunciating clearly.

The good news is Trombone has stopped barfing in my shoes, but L's are now the target. I try to tell L that means Trombone loves her.

I'm nearly done with my first semester—what a relief! We think L is going to get another project from Moon; she liked the work L did. The bonus was encouraging and her agent knows of another writer looking for a good researcher.

Sandy is a good gardener and my share of this year's harvest has been bountiful. We may go on doing that. She and T are good neighbors. Who knows, Ellie and Jersey might be happy together, too.

No more time. L needs me.